THE
ALLEGATIONS

April 7, 2020

Other Novels by Starr Sanders

The Boy Without A Face 2014

Pinkwashed   2017

DEDICATION

To my friend Nance Crosby whose courage, resilience and passion for life have been an inspiration to me

and

To Andy Silverman my husband and best friend forever.

THE ALLEGATIONS

A novel
By Starr Sanders

Chapter One

Yesterday, when I could look in the mirror and still recognize myself, was supposed to be the first day of the rest of my life. That's what they say when you turn sixty, isn't it? By this time you're already accustomed to the clichés around getting old, and you're expected to laugh every time someone makes a joke about being one step closer to the grave. Age is only a number, right? Still, you really do want to believe that big-number birthdays have a magical way of letting you reinvent yourself. Or at least letting you go ahead and fulfill your dreams finally. For as long as I can remember, I've wanted to be a judge. I did everything I thought was right. I got good grades. I went to Columbia. Then Georgetown Law. I worked my way up from intern to chief counsel for the Women's Rights Initiative, a women's sexual and reproductive advocacy group. I argued cases in front of the Supreme Court. I wrote a New York Times bestseller called Lady Justice.

I'm even a regular commentator on CNN. An actual

talking head. By all accounts, I have it all. Still: I've always loved the idea of bringing a room to order, of banging a gavel and becoming a vessel for justice, of making a difference.

Yesterday, I awoke with a lurch of excitement in my stomach, remembering Jules, my executive assistant, had heard from her friend over at the Department of Justice that my nomination was a go and the official call would come later that day. Political chits I had garnered with opposition senators over the years were finally paying off. I was on the verge of a federal judgeship appointment and I was on top of the world.

As I dressed for work, I attached to my lapel a tiny pin in the shape of Ruth Bader Ginsberg's collar of dissent. The miniature jewels sparkled. When I looked in the mirror, my eyes sparkled too. Yes, they were sixty-year-old eyes with all the crow's feet that entails, but this morning I loved them anyway. I thought about the week before, dashing to catch a flight at Reagan International, how I'd caught a glimpse of an advertisement for a private investment firm: *sixty is the new forty,* it said, over the image of a Robert Redfordesque guy perched at the edge of his sailboat, leaning into the spray. *Pfft,* I thought, hurrying past, *not MY poster boy.* What's ironic is that I am absolutely the demographic those investment firms are going after, but ads like that would never turn my head. Wouldn't you think marketing people could figure out that even older white ladies like me would be more inspired by an ad depicting a sixty-year-old woman of color taking on the patriarchy in high heels than an old white man on vacation showing us the size of his boat?

Still, I liked the idea, as clichéd as it might be. *Sixty is the new forty.*

Maybe now was the time to let my hair go a distinguished silver.

"All rise for the Honorable Judge Elaine Bower-Camden," I said to my reflection.

It's amazing the difference twenty-four hours can make. What a strange feeling to wonder who the person is looking back at you in the mirror.

The first time this happened to me was over thirty years ago, when a hairdresser cut off over a foot of unruly hair and I went from dishwater to platinum blonde. My then-boyfriend-now-husband's mother, Vivian, personally escorted me to her hair salon. I idolized Viv. She was the first woman ever to represent her district in the House of Representatives. I remember how starstruck I felt walking into the parlor with her. I was giddy as we linked arms. I loved feeling her top-of-the-line peach cashmere cardigan against my bare arm.

"Jean-Claude," she said to the stylist, leaning her hand warmly on his arm, "this is Elaine. She's my dear son's girlfriend and your job today is to make her look fabulous."

I was only dating Ted then, and he had never once called me his girlfriend.

To hear it from the lips of Vivian Camden made me dizzy with joy.

Jean-Claude led me to a chair and the two of them stood over me like a couple of Project Runway hosts, discussing the shape of my eyes (round, tending toward buggy), the path of my jawbone (distinct) and the height of my cheekbones (disappointing, but we work with what we have).

I didn't know then that Ted thought I was 'The One'. I didn't know that I'd marry him and that I would become the daughter-in-law of my idol. I only knew that I was enchanted by this polished woman I'd always hoped would run for the Senate and maybe even one day for President. I accepted without question all style directives she and Jean-Claude had in mind for me. I would have donned a polka-dotted clown outfit if Vivian said it suited me.

I knew then that I'd never again be me. I'd never again be little Lainey Bower, who wore a ponytail and ill-fitting sweaters. I didn't know yet about the downsides of the transformation I was about to undergo, and I'd never have dreamed about the upsides. Jean-Claude put a smock on me and turned my back to the mirror. Everything he was doing was mysterious. Vivian sat herself in the chair next to mine and told me stories about her early days in Congress. I felt as though I'd died and gone to feminist heaven.

We were in the salon for three hours. Vivian went out for French pastries while we waited for the hair color to set. The manicurist did her thing on my unruly hands, the makeup lady applied powders and creams and colors, and eventually they spun me around. Everyone applauded. I took in the sleek platinum bob and the makeup that didn't look like makeup and the eyebrows waxed into precise, subtle arches. As I looked, I felt as if I was peering at someone else. I thought: who is *that*?

Over the years, I answered that question by crafting a personality to go along with the looks. The beginnings of that personality, of course, had always been there. I was already ambitious, methodical, and passionate.

But the makeover — and, of course, Viv's attention — gave me the confidence to own it. I became, as my staff secretly calls me, Camera-Ready Camden.

I went 30 years without ever surprising myself, without ever wondering: *who am I?*

But, today — over 24 hours after my world was upturned — it happened for a second time. I walked by my vanity on the way to the freezer for more Mint Oreo ice cream. I caught my reflection and it startled me. I stopped before the mirror and studied the grubby tank I had been wearing ever since I retreated from the world to the safety of my house. I looked in disgust at the holey pajama bottoms covered in tiny popsicles and sundaes. I'd grabbed the clothes from a random drawer in our spare bedroom. They were probably my daughter's. I looked and I thought: *dear god, there is an old lady who needs some help.*

It's not just these gross pajama pants that are suddenly and inexplicably falling apart; it's everything — my family, my marriage, my career. *Me.*

It began with a phone call — just not the one I was expecting.

I never answer my own phone; that's what I pay my staff to do. To filter out the unnecessary. But I picked up because I thought it was 'The Call' about my nomination. Traditionally, the Attorney General phones the nominee to deliver the good news.

I was sitting at my desk eating a salad-in-a-jar when my office phone buzzed. I remember the salad because I told myself to remember it, to soak in every detail of what I'd been doing when I got the news that put me one step closer to my lifelong goal.

I cleared my throat, picked up my phone and did my best to contain my excitement.

"Mrs. Camden," asked a voice that was *not* the Attorney General's distinctive southern drawl. It was a voice I knew instinctively had rehearsed its lines; no one ever called me Mrs. Camden. I figured it must be a staffer.

"Speaking," I said, still giddy, still thinking '*It's happening! Finally! It's happening'!*

"What do you have to say about April McFarland's allegations against your husband, Ted?"

"The what …" I mumbled, feeling the salad start to rise in my throat. *The what?*

"Who is this?" I said.

She ignored me. "The allegations of workplace harassment? Sexual assault?"

"Sexual assau—" I repeated, then stopped myself, my training kicking in.

"I don't know anyone named April McFarland," I

said, ready to hang up as I realized *wait, do I?*

April McFarland. Could she be a former client? A former employee?

I had a flash of memory. About a month ago. A tall, lithe brunette dressed in black, ringing the doorbell of our home to drop off a box of files.

"Your husband's assistant?" the voice said. This was definitely a reporter, though in my state of shock I couldn't tell if it was the fidgety woman from *The Sun* or the wild-haired one from that snarky political website.

"Actually his colleague," I corrected her, despite myself. The one I clearly had not wanted him to hire.

"The allegations?" she pressed on, and now I could hear the self-satisfied tone of a hack journalist who knows she's just broken the news to a hapless victim and is reveling in the distasteful moment.

I remember now: *Elaine!* April McFarland said, placing the legal boxes on our doorstep like an offering and enthusiastically holding out her hand. *I've heard so many lovely things. I'm April.*

How could I have forgotten this name? I belched up salad greens and tangy dressing. I felt like the mousy girl who didn't know how to pick out a suit, the idiot who fell in love with some guy named Ted because she was enamored with his mother. I felt bumbling and naive.

But it only lasted a moment. I cleared my throat, thinking *I can retch when I hang up.* "No comment," I said to the reporter. "Ms. Bower-Camden has no comment."

Chapter Two

I ran to Jules' office in a fit of rage, embarrassment, and shock. Jules is my administrative assistant, my right and left hand appendage. We've worked in tandem over twenty years for the Women's Rights Initiative. She knows what to say and do even before I do. Before I open my mouth.

She was already on the phone when I got there. Her college roommate Henry, now a reporter at *The Post*, had already called her. She had him on speaker phone, her face a white expressionless mask. The reporter was telling her that my husband of nearly three decades, one of D.C.'s most renowned private litigators, a well-known personality in his own right, had been accused of sexual assault. They were going to run a story first thing tomorrow morning. Henry wanted a quote from me, and he was promising a balanced report, one that would contextualize the #MeToo aspects of the story as well as caution against a rush to judgment.

Hearing the classic perpetrator's caution against

believing women too quickly in reference not to some Hollywood smarmbag, but to one's own husband, is sobering to say the least.

"I appreciate this, Henry," she said into the phone. "I'll get back to you in twenty minutes."

"How could this be happening?" I asked when Jules hung up.

"You go home," she ordered. "Go home. Take a sleeping pill. Don't read the news. Don't check your email. And, whatever you do, *do not* contact Ted until we get to the bottom of this."

"Okay," I said, wondering how she expected me not to speak to the man who lived in my house. Jules called me a car. I got in without a word. I rode home in silence punctuated by frantic phone calls and texts from Ted, which I ignored. At home I sat on the couch in the noontime sunlight and watched the shadows deepen. Obviously, most women would believe their husband's tale of denial. My training and experience told me otherwise, especially regarding powerfully positioned men like Ted. And why not? He had been acting strangely, now that I thought about it.

Finally, I wrote Ted back: *don't even think about coming home.*

My phone vibrated again; I was declining all calls

but this one was the Department of Justice. I had, in fact, been awarded the nomination. The voice on the line wasn't the Attorney General, just an assistant. His announcement was perfunctory, mostly details on the confirmation process, with which I was already too well familiar, of course. The conversation was nothing like I'd built it up to be in my head. Funny how that works.

Here I am, still at home. Last night, I cried myself to sleep. This morning I woke up, and it's like someone moved my furniture a few inches in the night. Like the world is at a strange tilt. Mostly the same, but still all wrong. If Ted were innocent, wouldn't he have come over immediately – no matter what I'd said – to tell me I was wrong?

It's so strange to be in my house in the middle of the day. Actually, it's strange to be in my house when I'm not sleeping, wolfing down Greek yogurt, or reading case notes by lamplight in bed with Ted snoring next to me. I don't think I've stayed inside for more than a day since my daughter Kendall was born almost 30 years ago. Even then, I could only bring myself to take two weeks off work. Now I don't even know what to do with myself. I could probably go out, go for a walk around the neighborhood, or even go to Target. I'm bored silly and anxious with waiting, wondering, yet I can't bring myself to leave the house. I am keyed up and bone tired.

I feel absolutely sure that my husband would never cheat on me and wracked with suspicion at the same time. I feel totally certain he'd never assault anyone and equally convinced that women usually don't lie about assault. Why do I have such doubts?

I have never been unfaithful to Ted. I have never even considered it. I never needed to have an affair. Partly because I love Ted, for sure. But, also, partly because for years I have been cheating on Ted with my job. He knows I love my job, that it's his primary competition for my attention, and mostly he indulges my obsession. But he has his limits, and sometimes I'm not very good at knowing when I'm approaching them. My job beckons, and I come running.

My job is why, as soon as I heard the word 'allegations', I knew that my whole life was about to blow up. I've helped enough victims of sexual harassment sue their bosses to know that allegations mean trouble.

If I were a different woman, that word might not have made me sick to my stomach. I might have thought, *"well shit, my husband's assistant or whatever is really attractive, and he had an affair."* But I've spent my life helping women get legal recourse for the countless ways in which men – from bosses to boyfriends – have fucked them over. So I knew this situation was bad. Few reporters call the wife for comment when a rich white guy has an everyday affair with one of his subordinates. Okay, maybe they do, but it's not as newsworthy as this seems to be. I *knew* something bad had gone down and that this was going to be no ordinary allegation.

The phone rings again and it's Kendall. I don't know how to face her, and I've already ignored three of her calls. I have to answer.

"Mommy!" she cries. Her voice is hoarse, and I can tell she's been sobbing. "Where the hell have you been?"

"Oh, baby," I say. She is still my baby. She's 29 years old, and eight months pregnant with my first and perhaps only grandchild, but she will always be my baby, even if she marries that annoying soon-to-be father/boyfriend of hers. Even if her almost completed dissertation status at Georgetown becomes permanent.

"I'm so sorry," I tell her. "I just needed some…"

Some what? Some space? Some ice cream? Some time staring at the ceiling, saying 'fuck you, Ted'?

"I've been crazy worried," Kendall says. "I wanted to come by the house, but Jules says I can't go anywhere. She's got a security guard in my lobby!"

"Oh, please, honey. He's not security. He's probably an intern, someone to head off any media." Sometimes

I worry that my kid is so gullible.

"I can't believe what this girl is saying about Daddy. I can't believe she'd lie like this about him …"

"Oh, sweetie, I'm so sorry," I say.

I *am* sorry. I'm sorry that she's about to find out how complicated people are. I'm sorry that my daughter, naive enough to believe that my assistant has sent a bodyguard to her apartment complex, is about to learn such hard truths. I'm sorry to add stress to her pregnancy, which already hasn't been easy. Mostly, I'm sorry that I don't come to her father's immediate defense. I'm also sorry that I don't even want to.

"Kendall," I say, "I love you so much. You know that right? I love you and I love your baby and I'll always love your father because he gave me you." Uncharacteristically, she doesn't seem to mind that I'm treating her like she were thirteen years old. Pregnancy does weird things to your emotions. "But, honey," I continue, "I just don't feel like talking right now."

I don't feel like talking because I don't know what to say. I don't know how to tell her that my entire professional career is built on believing women like April, believing *women* in general. On knowing that as soon as a woman 'alleges', she's on trial, too. How can I throw all of that out just because I love my husband?

I convince Kendall I'm okay, neglecting to ask her how she's doing, if her ankles are swollen, if she's been drinking those dreaded protein smoothies. I tell her I'll call her back later. I feel badly but not bad enough to continue talking.

I flop backward onto the bed where I've lain underneath Ted so many times. I imagine him lying on top of this concubine, April McFarland, who is maybe four years older than Kendall. Then I imagine Ted lying on top of Jules. Then on top of several of Kendall's friends. I leap for the remote control to stop this line of thinking for a moment.

I turn on PBS just as Hillary Clinton is taking the stage at Wellesley for a women's conference on empowerment. I put on the closed captioning.

I take a deep breath and open my email. No unread messages. Thank god for Jules. I sort through my text notifications. The neighbors: *Are you okay? Let us know if we can bring over dinner.* A woman in my yoga class: *Breathe, baby, see you tomorrow.* Couple-friends checking in as diplomatically as possible: *Hey are you guys okay?* I don't have it in me to call any of them back.

I'm about to climb into bed and pull the covers over my head, but instead I find myself saying "Siri, call Ted."

"Calling Ted," Siri says.

"The number you have called is not a working number."

That can't be possible. "Siri, call Ted," I say again.

"Calling Ted," Siri says.

"The number you have called is not a working number."

That bastard. That prick.

I open my email, brushing aside the knowledge that whatever I send him will become part of a public and embarrassing record.

I compose a message. Subject: *You changed your phone number??*

Message: *You have a lot of nerve. You cowardly little shit. Your mother would be mortified.*

I tap "Send" and listen for the reassuring swoosh.

Then I turn up the volume on the television. Until this moment I hadn't even thought about Vivian. Ted's mother, my heroine. Living in her penthouse in Georgetown, having retired not to her home district of western Texas but to the place where she always felt most alive: the nation's capital. The heartbeat of America, she used to call it. For better or for worse. I really must go visit her as soon as possible. Tomorrow for sure.

Vivian is eighty-two years old and no longer in

the House, but she still wields considerable power on the DC social circuit. Her cocktail parties have been characterized on *Fox & Friends* as intellectual salons of liberal thinking where paid Black Lives Matter activists nibble on brie and baguettes while George Soros calls for more Chardonnay. Surely Vivian has heard the news by now. As my mentor, I know Vivian well enough to know that she will not reach out to me; she will wait for me to call. Furthermore, as my mother-in-law, I know her unapologetic tendency to leap to the defense of her precious son. This is not a conversation I am eager to have with her.

Hillary is talking about never losing your voice, never giving up. She's saying all the things she said that made the Women's Rights Initiative endorse her.

I think of how she must have felt when she heard about Monica and Bill or all the others.

I think of how I could look out my window right now and see no one.

There's no press at my door. There's no one following me trying to take my picture.

I think of how they're talking about Ted on television. They're mentioning me in the fine print, but the Women's Right's Initiative isn't headline news yet. We're being eaten alive in the comments section of an article in *The Post,* but it's nothing like what Hillary went through.

I'm just counsel for the Women's Rights Initiative, not the director, not the founder. I'm just a woman who landed a federal judgeship. I am just a woman married to the son of a popular former congresswoman.

A son who happens to be the attorney representing four complainants against hyper-right-wing family-values Senator Jimmy Montgomery, in a wrongful termination lawsuit. This was the case for which Ted had hired assistant counsel, April McFarland, to help with the extra workload. Ted's clients have all made allegations that the senator fired them when they became pregnant.

Allegations. There's that word again.

Mrs. Camden, what do you have to say about April McFarland's allegations against your husband Ted?

I think about Hillary losing the primary in 2012, finally securing the nomination in 2016 only then to lose to a Cheeto. I think about my client Elena Morales, who got a fifteen-year prison sentence for illegally possessing drugs belonging to her husband. She refused to share his name and whereabouts with the Feds, thereby declining the chance to save herself, an act of loyalty for which her husband rewarded her by getting another woman pregnant.

Hillary continues, "Don't let anyone tell you your voice doesn't matter," she says. "In the years to come, there will be trolls galore, online and in person, eager to tell you that you don't have anything worthwhile to say or anything meaningful to contribute. They may even call you a nasty woman."

I allow myself to cry only in the shower, so I stay in there so long that the water turns frigid. When I can no longer stand it, I stop crying. I shiver and I step out into the bathroom that is still steamy despite the cold water. I wrap myself up in a fresh, fluffy robe and breathe in the scent of something besides my sweaty armpits and rank pajamas.

I look at myself in the mirror, and I feel, for the third time now, like I don't recognize the woman reflected back at me. This time, it's different. She's not someone who shocks me with her glamour or startles me with her frumpiness and crusty eyes. I don't feel like I've lost myself.

I feel like I've found a new part of myself. This woman's skin is bare, wrinkled, loose, puffy around the eyes but clear from having cried out all her toxins. This woman is new to me. She's someone I'll have to get to know; we're in this together now.

I rub serum and primer on my aging skin. I switch

on the ionizing hair dryer and twirl my icy blonde hair around a jumbo round brush.

In the mirror behind me, I catch a glimpse of Ted's towel. I think of all the times I've tied his tie on the way out the door. I think of the way he kissed me goodbye Thursday morning before work. The last normal day of our marriage.

I apply mascara and lipstick and a dab of stupidly expensive French perfume. I look at the woman in the mirror – the woman who is both me and not me – and I know that we're both done holing up in this house, both sick to death of wallowing.

"We're going downtown," I say, shimmying into my most tasteful plum-colored shift and contorting to zip the zipper Ted has always zipped. "And we're going to make a public statement. We're going to say that we've already lost as much as we're willing to lose."

Chapter Three

It is freezing cold in the television studio where I'm preparing to give my statement. My good friend Adelaide Murphy's news show runs during the one o'clock hour on CNN and she's agreed to have me on for a three-minute segment.

I'm running a major risk by talking. For example, Jules is probably going to murder me. But I have to get out in front of this. I have to keep my eyes on the prize.

More than a year ago, when the judge currently holding the seat announced her retirement, I began lobbying senators. The judiciary isn't supposed to be political, but that's bullshit. Everything is political.

From the moment that reporter blindsided me with April's allegations, I knew there was a very good chance the scandal would cost me the judgeship. I used to get so mad when people called sexual assault allegations a scandal, but I guess things change when it's your husband being accused. I need 60 votes to confirm my nomination. I've initiated countless emails and phone calls, paid for dozens of luncheons. As a result of all that work and my qualifications, 59 are locked up, solid yeses, and I can't afford to lose them now. One – Jimmy Montgomery, Republican from West Virginia – is on the fence. Today on TV I'll have three minutes to reassure 59 senators that I'm still federal judge material and convince one in particular – Jimmy Montgomery – to vote *yes*.

Landing on an appellate court by way of a Republican-controlled Congress with a Republican in the White House is no easy feat. These 60 politicians are watching my every move. They're watching my professional performance, and they're watching my personal life.

It's infuriating, but it's also familiar. I can practically feel the smooth cool gavel in my hand. What would The Honorable Elaine Bower-Camden do?

She'd cut Ted out like a cancer. That's what I'm going to do.

I have a rule: when I shrug into one of my signature custom-tailored blazers, I cease to be a person and instead become legal counsel and talking head. I am neither wife nor mother nor lover. I am an object. I am a tool, a weapon.

The jacket I've selected for today is a shade halfway between suffragette white and the ecru of unbleached linen. I don't want to look like I'm wearing a lab coat, or worse, a tablecloth from the Plaza Hotel. I'm looking for something in between – something that says *luxury*, something that says *victory*. Most importantly, something that says *purity*. I straighten my dress. Under the jacket, the vibrant plum color I loved so much earlier now looks like the color of a bruise. Next to the not quite white of my jacket I cannot help but think of the creamy white thighs of April McFarland and the bruises she claims my husband left there. I know this because I stayed up much of the night reading and rereading every last word written about her allegations on the internet. Shivering in this overly cold studio, I feel my skin break into a clammy sweat and a wave of nausea washes over me. Can I really go on TV in a dress the color of bruises allegedly made by Ted's fingers? Ted's long, thick fingers?

Ted never had to worry about what he wore when he went on camera, which he often did. He could get away with a button-down shirt, sleeves rolled, giving his lawyering expertise an air of casualness as though he were simply born knowing the answers to complex hypothetical questions.

Can I do this? I have no choice but to do this. *Everything you've worked for is riding on this,* I remind myself.

"You look amazing," Adelaide whispers.

"Five-four-three-two and go," says the cameraman.

I plaster my Camera-Ready Camden face on as the blessedly hot lights shine down on me. I feel my clammy skin begin to dry. Years ago, someone told me to dab a little deodorant above my lip before I went on. It absorbs the sweat. At the time I was horrified, but right now I'm grateful for the tip.

"I'm here today with a dear friend, Elaine Bower-Camden," Adelaide begins. "She's here to talk about something very difficult. Elaine, there's no easy way to ask this," she says.

"There's no easy way to answer," I say, reciting the rehearsed lines I had anticipated and practiced in my head during the ride to the studio.

What I said is a blur. I leave the studio flustered and hot, happy for the frigid air outdoors. I'm seven years into menopause and by this time I am an expert regarding my hot-flash triggers. Red wine, dark chocolate, Ted's hands, performance anxiety. I have no reason to believe the show didn't go well enough, but there is an epic wave of anxiety heat, and I am frantic to get outside. Out on the sidewalk, I cool down and take the Metro toward home, enjoying the anonymity of the crowded car. When it hesitates between stops, I think about climbing out to street level and walking the rest of the way. But my stress level is suffocating. I stay put and ride it all the way to the stop closest to my house.

On the walk home I decide to get drunk and pig out and watch a recording of my segment. I order pizza online from We The Pizza and stop at Whole Foods for a bottle of Montepulciano and yet another tub of mint Oreo ice cream. I rush home in order to meet the pizza delivery guy.

Barely inside the foyer, I fling off my high black pumps. I throw my pristine blazer on the floor. I yank my bra off and uncork the wine. Some of it splatters onto my bruise dress, but I'm too emotionally exhausted to care.

The doorbell rings. I can already taste the pepperoni. I look in the front door camera to double-check that it's the pizza guy and not a reporter or something. Or, god forbid, Ted. I couldn't handle a contrite Ted right now.

Instead of dinner, all I can see is flowers. Practically a whole red rosebush.

So large that at first I can't even spot the pimply teenaged delivery boy until I open the door. I invite him in to set the arrangement on the table in the foyer. The display is huge, the kind of thing you'd buy for a funeral.

Or, in this case, the kind of arrangement you'd only send if you knew the recipient wanted to kill you.

"Somebody's sorry," the boy says, as I silently sign for the delivery.

Somebody's a sorry piece of shit of a husband, I think.

It fills me with a sick sense of pleasure to imagine Ted ordering the flowers before my segment. Not knowing that I was about to go on the air and ruin him. I picture the florist asking Ted what he'd like to write on the card. "What would you want to hear?" Ted would reply. He'd be at a loss. Good. I think of the millions of times I've signed birthday cards for his mother from the both of us. *We love you. We couldn't be luckier to have you. We are grateful every year for another year with you. All our love.*

I close the door behind the delivery guy, and walk the flowers into the kitchen. My body feels deflated, like a popped balloon. I hold onto the stems of the flowers as I pour out their water. I can't kill my husband, but I can kill these fucking flowers. I know it's morbid and a cheap metaphor, but I think of the great pleasure I'll get watching them shrivel.

I hate the smell of dying flowers, and Ted knows it. This bouquet is a power play. *He's good*, I think. He knows what I'm feeling. Even if he did send these after the segment, he knows I'm walking the walk: I'm following the advice I give my clients. You never want to believe the allegations when it's *your* man, I tell them. He knows I'm setting aside my heart — I'm closing it down — because when a woman makes allegations, I believe her. As much as I'd love to discredit April McFarland, use her youth and her long legs and blond hair against her, I've been doing this work long enough to know how unfair and misogynist that reaction is. My career has been based on the truth that #MeToo is teaching the rest of the world: when it comes to allegations of sexual abuse and harassment, women usually do not lie. Even as my heart is screaming to be let loose, to call my beloved husband and best friend and scream and yell and demand an explanation and pour out my pain and confusion, my head – thank god for my intellect! –is so far still in control. Yet, why don't I believe in him? Why don't I go in that direction? Easy. Anger and logic tells me otherwise.

Besides, there are only two ways the conversation can go: one, he could confess, and I'll have to leave him, and it will be ugly and public; or two, he could deny, and then I'll have to decide whether to believe that my husband is the one of the miniscule percentage of men who are falsely accused. And then convince the public I'm right. My options are shitty and I don't want to face them.

The flowers are fresh and lovely, and I can already smell the impending stench of their death. Ted has made the same move from the playbook of Senator Montgomery himself, the smarmy and disgusting defendant in the sexual harassment case Ted's currently litigating on behalf of four women clients who worked on the Senator's staff. Montgomery's habit of sending flowers to his victims turned out to be a common thread among them. I guess reading all of his clients' case files must have made an impression on Ted. I think about him poring over the Montgomery case documents in the office late at night, April McFarland at his side, her silk blouse just slightly too low-cut. Then I erase that image from my head: I'm falling into the trap of imagining a workplace romance told through the male lens, not an imbalance of power made dangerous by male sexual desire.

My lawyer instinct wakes up, and I am chastised: whether or not a woman's shirt is low-cut isn't relevant.

Among allegations of unsolicited flower deliveries, sexual harassment, and firing women for being pregnant, Senator Montgomery is also accused of sending unsolicited romantic notes. I think about Ted and April reading those notes together, what conversation they must have had about them, how raunchy some of them purportedly were, and how impossible it must have been to keep professional boundaries intact as the two of them sorted through the evidence.

Plus there was April's silk blouse to consider (*oh, stop it, Elaine!*).

I stare at the roses and wonder what sweet talk Ted instructed the florist to write on the card, but I don't have it in me to bother looking right now. I can't stomach hearing anything he has to say.

I put the card, unopened, into my briefcase. *I'll deal with that later,* I decide.

My phone buzzes. It's a text from Jules. She'll have seen the segment by now.

What. The. Hell. Were. You. Thinking.

Jules has attached the clip of my interview to her text message. I take a long sip of wine and stare at my phone. Finally I press the play arrow. There I am. Looking a little older and a little fatter than I feel when I look in the mirror, but good overall.

"I'm not going to talk about the allegations Ms. McFarland made about my husband," I tell the world. "I'm here to talk about what it means to be a legal professional. I'm here to talk about what it means to uphold the ethics and integrity expected of those in my job. I'm here to tell my husband: Ted, if you're listening, it's imperative that you tell the truth."

I wish I could claim that what I said was said out of anger. Passion. I wish I could claim I'd been caught up in the moment.

In reality, I said it because I needed to.

I made a deliberate, calculating choice. I selected my outfit. I prepared for my close-up. I let the makeup artist powder my face and coat my eyes with even more waterproof mascara that made them look bluer and more piercing. I put on my pearls. And then I fulfilled the nightmare of every male, politician or not, prominent or not, whose wife made the move that tanks careers.

I failed to stand by my man.

Chapter Four

The morning offers no respite for me. I'm tired and anxious, my mind overthinking what I'm feeling. Despite that, I have to go to court. I'm arguing the Elena Morales case. I rarely try cases anymore, but hand-picked this one wanting to right the outrageous injustice Elena has endured.

Jules, no doubt, is still livid with me and I don't blame her, so I decide to steer clear of the office before going to court. I call the makeup artist and stylist who usually preps me for television to come to the house instead. Before I became a talking head, I did my own damn hair and makeup for appearances. This time feels more important.

"Blot," she says, and hands me a Kleenex. The lipstick she has applied is exactly the same color as my tongue. She makes the dark circles under my eyes disappear. "There we go," she says, "ready for your close-up."

I wonder how many times in the course of her career she has said those words. She must say them at least as often as I say, 'I believe you; it's not your fault' or 'as your attorney, I have to advise you not to answer that'. I don't know if I'm ready to defend Elena as she deserves to be defended, but at least I'm prepared.

I've learned to fall back on that. It's what's gotten me through my most emotional cases. Practice. Preparation. Knowing every inch of a case, every deep dark secret about the client.

It has taken almost two years to have Elena's case remanded and retried. Two years in prison Elena has been away from her children. Two years incarcerated wrongly because of an improper search and seizure. This trial is a chance for Elena's redemption, and I need for the jury to believe in her innocence as well as her naivete. Easy to say.

Opening statements are tricky. You can't say too much. You can't portray the system itself as a massive failure because then you yourself are, well, part of the fruit of the poisonous tree.

Instead, you need another metaphor.

You need the jury to imagine justice as a well-oiled machine, chugging faithfully and efficiently along. You need them to think of the law as the track on which it runs. Sometimes a law is so bad it derails the whole thing, and the machine winds up in a ravine still chugging. Other times, the track simply runs in the wrong direction, cutting a path through a once-quiet neighborhood and disrupting all the lives. Yet no one outside the neighborhood really says anything until someone with a sympathetic story steps onto the track and gets run over by the machine.

My job is to make the jury understand that in this case, the law is a track that went the wrong way, a track that allowed the machine that is justice to roll over someone like Elena Morales.

"Plain and simple," I tell the jury during opening statements, "women often are guilty by association with the men they have chosen. Recent studies indicate that federal drug laws disproportionately harm women and people of color. Women like Elena Morales suffer. Women working hard to dig out of poverty often end up paying for the crimes of the men in their lives. In the last sixteen years over 2,000 Virginians have been incarcerated in federal prisons with mandatory minimum sentences ranging from five years to life without the possibility of release."

Sentencing is not usually an issue in the guilt phase of a trial, but I want the jury to understand the possible consequences of their verdict. Fortunately prosecutors rarely object during opening statements.

Their expert witness will no doubt defend the Reagan Era laws by saying "look, federal mandatory minimums don't affect *innocent* people. *Innocent* people don't get sentenced." I have to make sure that the jury knows that innocence isn't the issue. I learned a long time ago: as a woman, you can never call another woman innocent just because she was trusting and unsuspecting.

I try not to look at Elena's face while I'm speaking. I can't afford to break down. Never before have I empathized so much with a client, a radiology tech and single mom raising three kids ages five to thirteen.

Elena met her husband Jeff when she was a young divorced mother going to school full-time and waitressing on the side. She paid whatever neighbor or girlfriend she could to keep an eye on the kids and fell into bed for four hours each night bone-tired. Her ex had skipped town and disappeared years before, but Elena was not deterred. She worked at a coffee joint/ diner near the university in Albuquerque. She'd been strong. She'd been broken but full of pride, but now she was just broken.

After the government rested its case, it was our turn. With my own shitty husband on my mind, I put Elena on the stand.

"Ms. Morales, can you tell the jury how you met your

current husband Jeff?"

Technically, Elena and Jeff are still married. Even though Elena's rotting in jail and he's had a baby with another woman, and even though Elena's own children were sent by the state to live with Elena's sister in Pennsylvania when the father could not be found, the marriage continues.

I don't know why she hasn't divorced him. I've never asked her. I guess it doesn't matter who you're married to when you're behind bars. I think about Ted. I think: if he were convicted of sexual assault, would I stay married to him?

"I met Jeff when I was waitressing," Elena says. "Back in Albuquerque. We had this dish called Super Nachos. It was a huge plate, like a foot high. With chips and cheese and stuff ...."

"Relevance," opposing counsel shouts. He's eager, and young, and white. "Let the witness finish," the judge mutters. She's jaded, black, and nearing retirement. Her name is Nancy Jefferson. She's one of my favorite judges; we'd gotten lucky.

"Anyway," Elena says, "he used to order it, and I had to take it upstairs to him. Where he always sat. And one day he says to me 'it looks like you're real good at carrying things'. I should have known he was talking about me carrying drugs."

I've told her a hundred times that there's no way she could have known. Plus she certainly doesn't need to give the jury any ideas about totally blaming her for not knowing.

I look at my client, in the pale lavender button-down cardigan I bought her.

I think of everything that Jeff took from her. I think of the purple moons he left under her eyes. I think of the flood of relief and the trickle of pity she must have felt when he got the other woman pregnant and announced that he was leaving.

"Did your husband ever threaten to kill you?" I ask Elena.

"Yes," she says quietly, but is drowned out by the weak, nevertheless loud, objection of opposing counsel that is summarily silenced by Judge Jefferson.

"Yes," Elena says again. "He used to tell me all the time that if I left him, he would kill me."

"You weren't together anymore when he gave you the drugs," I said. "Why not?"

"He was actually living with Dolores," Elena says.

"Objection!"

"Overruled. You may continue Ms. Morales. But counselor, proceed cautiously," Judge Jefferson admonishes.

"And how is Dolores related?" I ask.

"Jeff and her had a baby...and she is pregnant again," Elena responds, eyeing the jury to gauge their sympathy. I'll need to remind her not to do that, even as I wonder, again, how society manages to judge mothers for having lots of kids but not the fathers who abandon them.

"So he's the one who left the relationship?" I say. "And he left the children?

Did he pay you any support or maintenance?"

"Actually he didn't leave," Elena says. "He stayed in our apartment because he said he needed room for his guitars. Dolores and the baby moved in, and he rented a studio apartment for me and the kids. The rent was late all the time.

Once when the landlady was on my back, he went and talked to her, and I never heard another word from her after that. Later I remembered that the next day I saw that somebody had hit her."

"Objection!" says the prosecutor. "Hearsay."

"Sustained," the judge replies. "Ignore that," she instructs the jury.

"Were you still afraid of him even after you weren't living together?" I imagine his death threats as a steady current of electricity underneath their relationship.

"It was worse afterward," Elena says. "He scared me even more. I couldn't calm him down like before. He was behaving just like he said he would if I ever left him. It didn't seem to matter that he's the one who left. I never even considered dating anybody else, oh my god! He would have killed me for sure if he found out. I felt like I still belonged to him and not in a good way. Like I was his car, or his dog."

"Tell me about the night he gave you the drugs," I say. "Did he tell you what he was giving you?"

"No, he gave me the suitcase and said if I messed with the lock he'd cut off my fingers. He said there was stuff inside he didn't want Dolores knowing about."

I think that Elena must have understood three things: 1. She was broken. 2. It had taken years to break her. 3. Dolores, who had a nine-month-old and was already pregnant again, wasn't broken yet.

I needed the jury to see all this, too.

Bit by bit we revealed Elena's story. She told Jeff that she would do it, she would hold the suitcase. It was locked and she never opened it, but she was no idiot. She suspected what was inside. But what could she do? Get rid of it, and risk Jeff killing her? She stashed it under her bed. Then, later, when the cops busted up his operation, Jeff told them that Elena had the product, that Elena was the go-between, that she was a mule for some guys in Colombia. They knocked on her door, and she thought that they were going to tell her that he'd died. Instead, they told her she was under arrest. Fortunately for Elena, in their eagerness, the police hadn't bothered to get a proper search warrant.

Elena must have felt the way I felt when the reporter called me. She must have felt her lunch rising in her throat. Must have thought there was a mistake. Must have slowly realized that she'd been betrayed.

Together Elena and I do our best to explain all of this to the jury. Who knows if they understand. Who knows if I understand.

Chapter Five

The judge calls for a two-day recess after one of the jurors becomes ill. I need the extra time along with the weekend. The guards bring Elena into a tiny private conference room in the courthouse so we can discuss her next round of testimony, only a few days away. It's five o'clock, early for dinner, but I know what Elena has to look forward to in terms of cuisine, so I offer to bring her takeout.

For some reason, Nance's Chili Bowl, located next to the courthouse, is her favorite. I normally try to never eat this kind of shit. But with Jules out of the picture for the moment there's no one to shove fresh vegetables in front of me. Ted is always whining about how I never let him eat at Nance's Chili Bowl. To think, all that time trying to keep the dumb motherfucker from needing gastric bypass surgery only to be forced to kill him because he couldn't keep his hands to himself and his dick in his pants.

"*I thought you hated that place,*" I can imagine Ted

saying as I dish Elena's chili out for her.

"*Hey! Guess what?*" I imagine myself retorting. "*It's possible that now I'm stuck with a rapist forever, so what does it matter?*"

My mind sticks on the word *possible*. I think of that movie *Boys on the Side*. After Drew Barrymore's character kills her boyfriend, Nick, she's in the getaway car with Whoopi Goldberg's character. "Oh, God. To think it's possible I killed my baby's daddy," Drew says.

"To think it's possible? You hit him in the head with a baseball bat," Whoopi informs her. "He's dead."

"No, I mean, it's possible that Nick is the daddy."

It's possible that Ted and I are stuck together forever. It's probable that he assaulted April. That's the truth that I settle on as I sit down next to Elena. She's looking at the notes I've scrawled on a large yellow legal pad. I've written *"Why should a woman pay for her husband's crimes just because they're married?"* and underlined it several times.

"Seriously," she says. "Why should we?"

"It seems to be the way of the world," I say, "but we're going to change that." Even as I say it, I doubt myself. I find myself being convinced we'll indeed change the world, while simultaneously wondering how on earth it could be possible that my husband is a predator.

Elena digs into her fast food with the gusto of a person who's been surviving on prison slop. I squeeze a plastic packet of sour cream onto the hot mess Ben's passes off as chili. I'm wracking my brain, thinking of every party I've ever been to with Ted, willing myself to sift through a mental file of possible signs that my husband is, after all, a sexual harasser.

Ted has always been something of a flirt, something of a benevolent sexist.

He's the type of man to refer to me as a 'girl' when he talks about how we met. He's the sort of man who says things like, 'well, women, y'all are too smart to go to war'. I've heard him lean into a Virginia drawl, the last vestiges of some tobacco plantation Southern Democrat with blue blood bubbling over when he needs to turn on the charm.

"The ladies in my section want me to ask you something," Elena says. "...in your section?" I say, before I realize she's using some kind of privatized prison doublespeak to refer to what we used to call a cell block. "Never mind," I say, before she can answer. "What ladies?"

She starts talking, telling me about some people named Sammy and Sally, who they are and why they are in jail. I can't concentrate on her story. I think of how I've tried to get Ted to stop referring to groups of women as 'ladies' and how Elena and her friends must find it a luxury to be called 'lady' instead of 'prisoner' or 'inmate'. Before he took the case against Senator Montgomery, Ted and I had talk after talk about how it's just as offensive to assume that women are perfect as it is to assume that they are sluts or baby factories. I told him women need to be allowed to be complex, three-dimensional. I believed that. I *believe* that.

Elena is getting to the point of her question. Sally and Sammy, it seems, are in some kind of trouble, a story having to do with one of their guards. He's been picking on them, bullying them. For some reason he's singled out Sally and Sammy among all the other lesbian couples in the place, and he's making their lives miserable with hateful barbs and random punishments, including keeping them apart.

Elena Morales and I have only about an hour to talk about her life, her case, her children, her testimony. But she wants to spend her time picking my brain on behalf of her friends. I'm continually blown away by the generosity of incarcerated women.

So why can't I concentrate on what Elena is telling me? I dig guiltily into my chili, stuffing another spoonful into my stupid mouth. Why am I having trouble viewing

April McFarland as anything other than a wanton vixen or an angelic virgin? Why do I keep reverting to an image of April in a leather bustier, trying to sleep her way to the top? Or a school girl, like Kendall, in her Exeter uniform walking home from class with her earphones in, just asking for trouble, just waiting to be grabbed by some sleaze or some murderer? Why do I keep seeing April McFarland through the male gaze?

"And so then they put Sally in solitary," Elena was saying. Something about the guard having caught her and Sammy holding hands and then Sally being flip with the guard. "It's totally fucked up because Sally is one of those people who really needs to be around people, you know? She gets super depressed, it's not healthy."

Why can't I see that April McFarland — like every woman, like Elena Morales, like me — can possess a multitude of character traits? Can't Elena be the sort of woman who works her way out of poverty and cooks her children organic meals and launders her lavender towels every other day and yet also goes to prison for storing her ex-husband's drugs under the bed? Can't she be a woman like me, who can love her husband and love her child, but love her job more, love her career so much that she'll do whatever it takes to save it?

Women deserve to be complicated. Even April.

I nod and grimace at Elena as she goes on with her story, listening halfway, choking down my frustrations along with gulps of chili. It seems that when Sally was in solitary for a week, her girlfriend Sammy formulated a plan that involved somehow getting this guard in trouble with his boss. I don't pay much attention to the few details, but it sounds like the whole scheme is tragically farfetched, not to mention dangerous.

"Sounds like your friends are playing with fire," I murmur.

I wonder how long Ted has been sleeping with April. Was he sleeping with her when I was at work, trying to explain institutionalized sexism to some obtuse reporter for the seven hundredth time? During the day while he held me at night? Was he texting her while I lay in his lap sobbing on election night, when Hillary didn't win and I whispered into the pleated crotch of his pants, wet from my tears, that I felt like I was at America's funeral? That I felt like the election had been a referendum on gender, and that women had lost?

Was he sleeping with her then? Or was he assaulting her then? Or was he sleeping with her and then assaulting her?

I don't have any of these facts, plus I'm not making any sense, so I return to the ones I do have, to the literal pile of facts in my briefcase. Someone else's facts. I pull out Elena's file as a signal we should shift the subject away from Sally and Sammy and start talking further about her testimony.

I open the file and something falls out.

It's the card from Ted that came with the flowers. Suddenly it's imperative that I know what it says.

"I'll be right back," I say, "you enjoy your supper."

As I leave, the guard stationed outside who's assigned to Elena rolls his eyes at me. The expression on his face is overly familiar and annoying. Why does he assume I'm on his side?

I feel like I'm going to be sick. I take the card with me to the restroom at the end of the hall. I feel the chili start to rise in my throat, but it stays put. Thank god. I sit on the toilet to catch my breath. Then suddenly I'm thinking of the times Ted rubbed my back while I barfed from morning sickness. I knew he was behind me, disgusted, but, still, he stayed.

I slide my fingers under the seam of the envelope and tear it open.

My contacts are cloudy from tears, but I can still make out the florist's clean, precise print. It says: *How could you, Elaine? She's lying.*

When I recover from my bathroom breakdown

and return to Elena, I blurt out something I've been meaning to ask her for ages. "Do you think you'll ever forgive Jeff?"

She looks at me. Her eyes well with tears. Then she laughs.

"What the hell's the point of being mad at a man?" she asks. "You don't get mad at a dog for being a dog, do you?"

I don't know whether to laugh or cry. I don't know what to make of my client rotting in jail and refusing to be angry about it and even advocating for her friends inside, when I've spent the last 48 hours doing nothing but stew.

"Anger will eat you up," she says. "That's what I tell Sally and Sammy. I try not to get angry because I don't know how to stop it once it starts. I try to think of the good stuff. Or at the least the okay stuff. The way Jeff would get up in the morning with the kids so I could take my time doing my makeup. He'd buy me Skittles at the gas station."

I open her file again, ready finally to get to work. "So," I say, moving us along, "your friends Sally and Sammy. They wanted you to ask me something?"

"Never mind," Elena says, and even though I know she doesn't mean it, that she wants to keep telling me about her friends, there's nothing I can do about a homophobic asshole prison guard, and she can see it on my face. So like a distracted harried female attorney with a cheating lying rapist husband, I say, "okay, let's talk about your testimony when you return to the stand on Friday."

Elena shoots me a disappointed look, and we move on.

Chapter Six

I go home to my empty house. My cell phone is still off. I power it on and call Ted.

Still, his number has been temporarily disconnected.

Not thinking, I send him a text. '*You coward. At least pick up the phone*'.

The text returns, number disconnected.

I need to call Vivian. His mother, my mentor. In any other similar situation, a crisis that didn't involve her son and where he was or wasn't putting his penis, I'd have had her on the phone within an hour, seeking advice. But this time I don't want to hear what she has to say.

I'm standing in front of the open refrigerator when the doorbell rings.

It's Kendall. I let her in and she clings to me, trembling. She's not due for another three weeks but her belly is enormous.

"What the fuck, Mom," she says, the minute she lets go. "You think it's okay just to ignore me?"

"I'm sorry, sweetie," I say. "I'm just…"

"What? I'm just what?"

"It's been a really long day." Had it only been the previous day that I was on television?

"—and Dad? Why won't you call him back?"

"Call him back? I've been trying to get through to him, he disconnected his phone—"

"Of course he did, what do you expect? The media are going crazy—"

How did I raise such a sensitive kid?

"So you've spoken to him," I say.

"Yes, Mom, I've spoken to him!" She sounds like she's seventeen, but I don't dare say that to her. "The question is, why haven't *you?*"

When I was pregnant with Kendall, I wanted to name her Jeannette, after Jeannette Rankin, the first woman in Congress. Ted had *hated* the name. He thought it sounded like a grouchy schoolmarm. When he wouldn't let me have that, I lobbied for giving the baby a hyphenated last name. He hated that, too.

In the end, we reached a compromise on a trip to Boston during a power outage on the T. We'd had another fight over names, and I'd gone to sit alone.

Then the train plunged into darkness. My biggest fear of city dwelling was being caught in the subway and having to get out of the train, crawling through a tunnel full of rats and god knows what else.

Ted knew that, of course. Before I could scream or cry or yell for him, I felt him beside me, his hand in mine. We sat there in the dark, each minute seeming like an eternity. Ted said 'breathe' and I breathed. I remember so clearly inhaling and feeling my pregnant stomach rise and fall. Then the lights came on just as suddenly as they'd gone off. The train lurched forward and came to a stop.

At Kendall Street Station. The doors opened and the conductor announced the station.

"Kendall," he said.

"Kendall, we have never been so happy to see you, Kendall."

Four and a half weeks later, I gave birth to our daughter, and we called her Kendall Rankin Camden. A little something for everyone.

Now she is pregnant herself. If her child is a boy, she'd already chosen the name Steven, after her boyfriend's father, which I found boring as hell and felt depressed every time I thought about how many times in my lifetime I would have to pronounce that truly average word. *Steven.* I hoped my grandson would turn out to be more exceptional than the name they'd be giving him. Or at least as exceptional as his mother. I am so crazy about that girl.

"Dad's seen the interview you did this morning, in case you're wondering," Kendall says. "He's beside himself."

Beside himself? I wondered. I tried to imagine Ted that agitated and found that I couldn't.

How could you, Elaine? She's lying!

"Listen, honey," I say. "I'm not having a particularly easy time of this either."

"It would be easier if you'd call him," she says, waddling down the hallway toward the kitchen. "Do you have anything to eat?"

I love my child, and I love that she's pregnant, and I would love nothing more than to curl up on the couch and talk about her lovely baby shower last weekend and the wallpaper in her nursery and listen to her worries about her condescending obstetrician or whether her boyfriend will faint at the first sight of blood. What a luxury it would be, I find myself thinking, to have back the normal life we were all living a few days ago.

Now all I want is for Kendall to leave. I want to pour a huge glass of wine and eat popcorn for dinner.

But she's not going anywhere. She's been stewing over her parents' marriage and possible divorce all day, and she's determined to make me listen. I follow her down the hallway toward the kitchen.

"Has it occurred to you that the accusations might be false," she asks opening the refrigerator. "This is Daddy we're talking about!"

"They're all someone's daddy," I reply, regretting immediately the double entendre and noting with relief that Kendall doesn't catch it. She pulls out a leftover carton of Chinese food, sniffs the contents, and puts it in the microwave.

"Don't give me that whole routine," she says, watching the carton rotate. She's wearing one of her crazy floral jumpers, and her abundant straight black hair is secured in a haphazard bun atop her head.

"I'm not one of your clients, and neither for that matter are you. Tell me something, would you follow your own advice? If you were your client, would you actually believe your lawyer when she says your husband definitely slept with his intern—"

"—assistant counsel," I correct.

"—even though said lawyer has never met your husband? Knows absolutely nothing about him? Has no idea about what goes on in your relationship? Even though your lawyer has a completely skewed perception of reality because she only sees the worst cases? She never actually meets the people who have worked out their problems, obviously. Thus her advice—the advice you're giving yourself right now and apparently taking — isn't based on reality at all. The reality is that the great majority of marriages actually *survive* crises like this."

The problem with sensitive children is that they're ridiculously perceptive. I don't know what to say to this, so I go to the fridge to find the wine. The microwave dings. Kendall takes the carton and a fork to the couch and picks up the remote control. Does everyone revert to a teenager when they go home? It occurs to me to be thankful that Ted didn't let me name this child Jeannette. I put a bag of popcorn in the microwave and pour myself a glass of Chardonnay as it expands. I join Kendall on the couch, where we watch two recorded episodes of Desperate Housewives before she falls asleep, snuggled against me and snoring like a baby.

Before this horrible week, I liked to think of Ted and me being the sort of couple who knew everything about each other. In fact, I'd often joke that we were married because we knew too much.

"If he ever leaves me," I'd say to friends and colleagues, "it's mutually-assured destruction."

Time has a way of making everything ironic.

The truth was more complex. Our marriage was like any marriage that had lasted. It was messy. Our closeness ebbed and flowed. Sometimes we were so close that Ted felt to me almost like a 232-pound appendage. Other times, he felt ever-so-slightly distant. Just mysterious enough to be exciting. It felt as if he were constantly darting just out of my reach and the chase was thrilling. I'd savor it, the way one enjoys a rich dessert, by removing his clothing and straddling him just before he left for a morning meeting.

There were times (lots of them), that I thought my life would be easier without him. When I considered putting all of his stuff in trash bags and hauling it to the curb. When I considered getting in my car and never coming back. There were times when I was his biggest fan and times when I desperately wanted credit for his success. There were times that I envied him. My ambition was often stifling even to me. Ted took the brunt of it all.

Lately, our relationship — if you can still call it that — had felt more strange than distant. More unfamiliar. The further he drifted from me, the more indifferent I felt. I've been wondering recently if this was a protective defense mechanism for both of us. Perhaps, on some intuitive plane, he knew that I was slowly but surely phasing him out of my career decisions. Perhaps, he sensed that as I went through menopause and Kendall required less and less of my devotion, some of the attraction and affection I felt for him had begun to erode.

Perhaps, he missed the days when whatever emotion I felt for him, even the negative ones, was loud and intense. Perhaps, he too had decided to continue to lower the volume.

That's all speculation, of course. As for the facts: I was hiding something from him. My lie of omission began the way every lie does. I wanted to hold onto something important to me. No, it wasn't just that I wanted to. *I needed to.* The deception started the first time Ted mentioned taking the case against Senator Montgomery, *The* Jimmy Montgomery. But the story started long before that.

"I've pretty much decided on doing it," Ted said. We were having a rare night at home, making a pasta carbonara. I'd suggested the decadent meal as treat to celebrate his birthday a little early since he'd be away on business on the actual day. Jules would have scolded me if she knew I was eating bacon.

"Doing what?" I asked, thinking he meant eating the entire four-pound allotment of the $8.99 a pound bacon

I'd bought. It turned out that what he really meant was even more disturbing.

"Taking the case against Montgomery."

Shit, I thought. "Don't do it," I said, making a well in the large mountain of flour on the counter. I needed to keep my voice even. I had to hide how much his statement alarmed me. "It'll be a nightmare."

"I think I have to," Ted said.

"It's a bad idea," I said, cracking eggs into the well. "You know you're not going to win. Montgomery will find a way out of it. Plus, you despise his lawyer, Mel Malone, who you know represents anyone for a price. And he's damn good at doing it."

"Everyone hates Mel Malone. That's true. But that's no reason not to take it," he said, laying thick strips of bacon on a sheet pan. Normally I'd have yelled at him for not lining it with tinfoil first, but I needed to throw him off taking the Montgomery case, and I had to think carefully, so I let it go. I could buy a new sheet pan.

Ted was right about Mel Malone. If no one would take cases against him, every rich white man in the country would have an even bigger and blanker check to do whatever the hell they wanted. Malone had made a name for himself with underhanded tactics and unethical moves as slick as his greasy hair.

I also needed to emphasize to Ted, though, that nothing good could come from battling Malone in court, or, in the more likely scenario, dealing with him outside of court to reach a settlement. My staff liked to call him "Going Straight to Hell Mel." He had an over-large mouth full of over-large teeth and wrinkled leathery skin.

"Um, have you *met* Mel?" I asked. "Have you not seen his work in Ghostbusters?"

"He *does* look like Slimer," Ted laughed. He was a huge Belushi fan and loved to play the cult classic as background for boring work. He slid the sheet pan into the oven then took his phone from his pocket to do a Google image search. "Oh my god, it's *uncanny*." Our sense of humor was intact.

"Right!" I began to knead the pasta, and the movement was therapeutic. Thinking of the mere possibility of my husband taking the case against Jimmy Montgomery gave me the urge to manhandle something. Yes, Montgomery needed to be taken down, no question, but let someone else's husband alienate the senator. Someone who doesn't need his vote for a federal judgeship.

"The mouth!" I cackled. "The hands, too!"

For a brief time in the early 2000's, Ted and I saw a

marriage counselor.

She told us that there is one fundamental source for all tensions between married couples. As lawyers, we'd immediately shut down at the thought of only one possible universal explanation for anything. We never went back.

We were probably right to reject something so simplistic, but the history of our marriage will more than likely validate her premise. I think of her words often. She said "men need everything spelled out, so they feel confused when women resent having to be so direct and explicit. As a result, men bumble along boundary-less until they stumble over the landmines of women's unspoken expectations."

I hated hearing it. But I did often resent Ted for needing to be told. He often complained that I blow up instead of telling him what I want.

This exact scenario played out that evening in our kitchen. I skirted the issue. I should have told Ted, "I want that federal judgeship, and I'll need Montgomery's approval to get confirmed, so please don't take the case." Instead, I just got mad that Ted didn't know this without my telling him.

Honestly, he should have known. I was constantly bitching about how Bill's inability to keep his dick in his pants or his goddamn crime bill was going to sink Hillary's nomination. Two days before in bed, I'd read out loud from a girlfriend's op-ed in the *Wa Po* entitled 'Hey! Stop Blaming Hillary for Bill's Mistakes!' I'd gone on a long diatribe about how the female half of a high-powered couple can't separate herself from her husband's public behavior.

Ted should have connected the dots. He should have asked instead of telling me. He should have thought about me without being asked. For once.

Chapter Seven

An empty stomach is not good for a political career, and no one on Capitol Hill understands that better than the family who owns the Monocle. It doesn't matter who's in charge of Congress, this old stand-by restaurant is a favorite venue for fundraisers, caucuses, and, of course, shrewd negotiations. When a gun bill or immigration bill is on the House or Senate's docket, it's utterly impossible to get a table.

That's why I don't think twice about meeting Frank Francis at the Monocle. D.C. insiders — and Senator Frank Francis is the *epitome* of a D.C. insider — like it because, frankly, 'what happens at the Monocle *stays* at the Monocle'. Many an unoriginal restaurant critic has grabbed onto the low-hanging fruit of its name, making the joke that the staff "turn a blind eye" to the inner goings-on of our deeply flawed government.

This behavior isn't unique on Capitol Hill, of course. No restaurant could stay in business if it didn't keep a heavy hand on its staff to be quiet. The rule is as institutional as the Supreme Court and the Capitol Rotunda. *Don't talk.*

Don't talk about the senators who sit way too close to women who are not their wives. Make no mention of congressmen who vote against Planned Parenthood funding in the afternoon then spend the evening over stiff Old Fashioneds with a mistress, openly discussing her upcoming abortion. Don't talk about the lobbyists and their lobster tails. Blue Cross Blue Shield was never here. The National Rifle Association shoots its own meat and thus has no need for your fine establishment. When you deliver a plate of pan-fried crab cakes to table seven, that man may look like a candidate from the 2008 election, but pretend he doesn't. Donald Trump Jr. and a guy with a Russian accent were definitely *not* in your reservation book.

What was surprising is that Frank Francis called me at all. On the office white board where I tracked which Senators I could count on for my confirmation, I'd relegated Senator Francis into the squarely "no way" zone. Certainly his call was related to my television appearance yesterday, but how?

I was shown past a row of deep red leather booths with high upholstered dividers to an even more discreet booth near the back of the room. Bushy ferns hung everywhere as discreet privacy blockades. Does Francis have a regular table, I wondered? I ordered a glass of wine as I waited. Where was the logic in this? Why would what I had said on CNN make him suddenly want to support my candidacy for the judgeship?

Elena Morales may not spend her time dwelling on why she ended up where she did. But I, like every lawyer, am obsessed with cause and effect. I've spent hour upon hour digging for the root of Elena's calamity. Now I'm doing it with my own calamity.

In law school, I learned there are only two types of causation: cause-in-fact and proximate cause. Cause-in-fact, the relationship between cause and effect, is determined by the *sine qua non*—Latin meaning "*but for*"—test. But for someone's conduct, the result would not have happened. Cause-in-fact is endless.

But for Ted taking Senator Jimmy Montgomery's case, he would not have needed to sort through an avalanche of phone records and affidavits and more emails than Hillary Clinton's.

But for Ted needing extra help, he would not have hired April McFarland.

But for the late hours and the close proximity, Ted would never have learned her name.

But for the enormous amount of work it takes

to help prosecute a sitting senator in a high-profile discrimination case, Ted would never have suggested that they make it a late night.

But for the fact that both he and April were starving, Ted would not have ordered them takeout.

But for the fact that Ted felt guilty for asking April to stay late and miss a friend's birthday party, Ted would never have suggested they open a bottle of Clos Fourtet Bordeaux 2015 from the case that a client had sent.

But for the fact that they didn't want to waste an uncorked bottle of wine, they wouldn't have finished it.

But for its pure floral aroma, giving way to ripe and stylish plum and boysenberry and blackberry, they would never have opened a second bottle.

But for the fact that Ted had once mentioned it was my favorite, the client would never have thought to track it down.

But for, But for, But for.

Sine qua non …

Cause-in-fact is endless. Therefore, that's what proximate cause is for. It's a legal limitation to infinite possibilities. It's a way to find your way back to the beginning of a story of wrongdoing. As I sit sipping my wine in this quiet corner, I manage to prove to the judge in my head that the proximate cause of my marriage crumbling is the self-righteous morality of Senator Jimmy Montgomery.

Like Senator Montgomery, Senator Frank Francis is a soulless corporate crony and founding member of the Good Ol' Boys Club. Unlike Montgomery, Frank and I dated, twice, in college.

He's a Republican dressed in a Libertarian suit, and I hate him. I've been avoiding him, actually. But now that I've lost Senator Montgomery as a vote for sure, Frank Francis is a chance to save my career. So, when he calls as I'm getting on the Metro for work and invites me for drinks, I say yes.

But for my confidence in tradition, I would never have said, "Okay, let's do it."

But for the part of me that resented Ted for taking the case against Jimmy Montgomery and losing me his vote, I would never have said, "Yes, this evening will be fine."

But for a possibly subconscious desire to get caught, I would never have been photographed in the dark with Frank Francis.

Sine qua non.

I'd be lying if I said that my need for a 60th vote wasn't on my mind when I agreed to meet Frank for drinks. I'd be lying, too, if his stunning face and sexy grin weren't also on my mind. Our college fling was common knowledge among our social and professional circles, and nobody cared — Frank and I were done and over in the blink of an eye, forty years ago. Still, the rumor mill being what it is, and Frank's political stance being so morally repugnant, I knew it would be best if we weren't seen together. I suggested that maybe meeting in public wasn't the greatest idea.

"Don't be silly," he said, and I acquiesced.

I didn't think meeting with Frank would have actual public relations consequences. I thought I'd just get a chance to fantasize about the look on Ted's face if we were to be caught. I thought maybe worst-case scenario, a friend-of-a-friend would tell Ted. It's not like reporters follow me everywhere or anything.

Was this what Ted thought when he did whatever he did with April McFarland? Did he do it half because he could and half because the idea of me finding out was a thrill?

It's not me I should be worried about, obviously. It's Frank Francis. When a member of Congress preaches family values out of one side of his mouth, and, according to the rumor mill, visits gay bathhouses with the other, it's likely that local gossips will care who he has drinks with.

Senator Frank Francis's secret life was an open secret among the D.C. gay conservative community, but even those guys were losing patience with his hypocrisy. Given that my work at the Women's Alliance brings us into partnership with all manner of identity groups and the late-night cocktail parties that entails, I knew of Frank's reputation. When I heard, I was shocked for exactly four seconds, and then it all made sense. His intolerance, his obsession with traditionally masculine behavior. That fundamentalist father of his.

Given his enthusiasm for hetero sex — believe me, sex with Frank was nothing if not enthusiastic — I'm certain Frank Francis isn't gay. A closeted raging bisexual? This I believe, without question. Wife and kids, vanilla life in public; leather boys and kink in private. In college, he was known by everybody as just a sex machine. This was in the seventies; he had long hair, he wore bell bottoms, he listened to Led Zepplin. He was too beautiful, too charming, too dripping in pheromones to be resisted. When he turned his attention to me, I was in shock and awe, which is why we lasted for even a second date. I was seduced by that face, that body, those perfectly straight white teeth.

Frank caught the eye of men, too, and he would notice it. He would mutter *faggot* under his breath when certain men passed. I wouldn't be surprised if there had been some experimentation happening back at the frat house.

I have no idea whether Frank Francis realizes today how close to the edge he is currently living, how open his secret really is. I wonder how many years he has been lying. I wonder if he has any idea that I know.

I've always had a type, and dating Frank in college helped me realize which kind of guys fit me and which did not. I've never been too moved by his kind of power. I value charm and self-deprecation, a guy who tries to be chivalrous, but winds up being a little oafish. I'll take a public defender in a rumpled button- down who forgets his wallet when he takes me out to dinner over a senator in a $700 tie. When it comes to romance, I don't like being chased or hunted. I like being adored.

Nevertheless, when I sense Frank's presence and look up from my phone to find him standing over the table, I feel something stir. It starts in my stomach, like the flitting butterflies I felt in the presence of my handsome high school English teacher.

I stand to greet him and take in his dapper presence. He's wearing a crisp charcoal gray suit and a baby blue pocket square, the picture of a Southern gentleman. What Kendall would call a silver fox.

The confident way he moves overtakes me, and — I admit it — I am aroused. A wave of sexual excitement and a familiar feeling of forbidden attraction wash over me. *Settle down, Elaine,* I think, *this is a no-no.* This is the impulse that makes 20-year-old undergrads sleep with 62-year-old professors. This is what leads interns to make bad choices in the Oval Office. Maybe this was what got Ted in trouble?

If I were a different kind of woman, I think. But I've never been that kind of woman. I am here for one reason and one reason only: to make a deal. If I were to have any hope for the judgeship, I need Senator Frank Francis's endorsement. Period. I am ready to do whatever it takes. Almost.

Frank holds my forearms and pulls me in for a hug, a power move that says, *you belong to me.* I tense up against his touch and remind myself that this balance will be delicate. I will need to let him slide on a few things in order to get what I want.

I let the hug linger slightly longer than a hug with a senator should. We scoot into the horseshoe booth, and I stop on my side; Frank keeps going, sliding closer to me, and winds up in the middle, positioned like a Mafioso with an anonymous female stuck to his hip. The waiter arrives, and Frank orders our drinks.

"The lady will have a vodka martini," he says and winks at me. "Make it dirty, too. Grey Goose. Extra olives. Same for me."

Oh, god, I think, *he's winking. He's ordering our old college drinks. This isn't going to end well.*

"So, dear," Frank says, leaning in to touch my arm. "Shall we wait for our drinks, or shall we simply cut to the chase?"

"I don't know about you, but I'm free to linger for a bit," I say.

"I've got all night," he says, laughing and letting his gaze fall to my neckline, a neckline I chose precisely because I want to be a federal judge.

Chapter Eight

This isn't the first time I've tried the neckline strategy. Six months ago, well before Senator Montgomery's employees went public about his workplace behavior and harassment, well before he became Ted's client, I went through this same ritual, in this same restaurant, at another table, but this time with Senator Montgomery himself, the potential 60th vote. After that meeting, I went straight back to my office and shifted his name firmly into my "no way in hell will I get his vote" column of my white board. I never suspected that his name would come back into play sooner than I thought.

I had delivered the same line to Jimmy Montgomery at the Monocle that I had used on Frank Francis just now.

"I have a little while to linger Senator," I said.

"Excellent news," Montgomery replied, addressing my neckline. "Me too."

"Oh?" I said. "Is Lorelei down in Houston, then?"

Lorelai Jennings Montgomery was the senator's third wife, 22 years his junior and a Texas beauty queen. She had four children, one after the other. They had married three weeks after the senator's second wife, Helen, succumbed to breast cancer. The guy was a real peach.

"She's with the kids," he said. "How old are they now?" I asked, hoping that the mention of his family wouldn't backfire, making him feel guilty for flirting with me. Not that men like Jimmy Montgomery were even capable of guilt.

"Two, four, six, and Jamesie, the boy, who's seven." He produced his phone from his breast pocket and handed it to me.

"You old so-and-so," I said, "you're sure keeping her busy!"

I felt his foot inch toward my foot and stop, barely touching mine. I smiled harder than I needed to at the photograph of the woman who could be his daughter and, who, if I'm not mistaken, is younger than his son and daughter from his first marriage. She was surrounded by four tow-headed tots. She'd maintained her stiff pageant coiffure and thick makeup for the photo, but even that couldn't hide the sleep deprivation. I think her life would have killed me.

Lorelai Montgomery's first pregnancy had made headlines, but not in the way one might think. Sure, the Senator and his third Mrs. had taken a crap on decorum, barely waiting for the ink to dry on Helen's death certificate before announcing their whirlwind engagement. Yes, they'd had a shotgun wedding for 500 guests. Yes, they'd passed the one-year anniversary of poor Helen's death in the hospital maternity ward. The Montgomery family had made headlines, all right. But it wasn't for any of their lousy behaviors; Senator Montgomery is the ultimate spin doctor. Instead of a scandal, their new baby was presented by the media as a miracle. The sins of Senator and Mrs. Jimmy Montgomery were absolved. They had given the Christian right a precious gift: a chance to speak up for the "pre-born."

One afternoon, Senator Montgomery received a call that the *New Daily News* was about to go public with his mistress' ill-timed extramarital-to-anyone-who-knows-math pregnancy. Within twenty minutes — in keeping with what was clearly a public relations emergency plan — Lorelai was on the set of Fox News primetime in a baby blue suit announcing their engagement and cradling her tiny baby bump while dabbing her eyes with a tissue.

"We're choosing life," she said. "We do not believe that the Lord makes mistakes, and we are committed to being parents to baby Jimmy. The Bible says I knew you before I formed you in your mother's womb. Before you were born I set you apart and appointed you as my prophet to the nations. We trust in God's plan for our baby."

I wanted to know what kind of god presents a plan in which people can name their child Jimmy Montgomery. Junior.

All those years of beauty pageants had paid off. Lorelai expertly shared the story of a "diagnosis" of "complications" that had prompted her OBGYN to beg her to abort, allegedly comparing Sweet Baby Jimmy Junior to a tumor that might kill her. For weeks before the birth she went on the Evangelical speaking circuit.

"A diseased clump of cells!" she told the crowd gathered for the 28th annual National Memorial for the Pre-Born. My staff found the video on YouTube. "Can you believe that's how they referred to my little miracle?" Lorelai rested a hand on her belly, flashing a gaudy chunk of diamond. "The doctors told me that he'd suffer if I let him live, that killing him was the only humane choice, but I serve an awesome God, a God too big for the limits of modern medicine. My little Jimmy healed in the womb by his maker and not only did God work his heart, he worked *my* heart too. Now, I have the incredible privilege to be the voice for those preborn babies who have no voice of their own."

In this way she and Jimmy Montgomery deflected entirely the question of his infidelity to a wife dying of cancer. Patient confidentiality of course prevents us from knowing if their obstetrics horror story was indeed the fabrication of which it reeked. It helped them, of course, that we're living in an era where lies trump truth.

I'm sure that none of this had anything to do with her husband's lifelong quest to defund Planned Parenthood.

Nope, nothing at all.

"They're darling," I said to the picture the senator held at me to admire. "Junior is doing well?"

"Jamesie as we now call him, and yes, he's a handful," Senator Montgomery said. "They all are. They sure keep her on her toes."

"I bet they do!" I said. For good measure, I threw in "just like their daddy? Motherhood is the most important job a woman can do!"

Looking back, I can imagine him saying this to his staffers before he fired them for getting pregnant.

The waiter arrived with our drinks. I took a long swig

of mine, reeling from its potency.

"Any plans for number five?" I asked.

"Oh, who knows what she's got planned," he said, and winked. Oh lord, I thought, it's like they know their role down to each stupid gesture. "You ladies always have a plan, don't you?"

I giggled, hating myself for it. "Wow, you're not even going to let me finish my drink first?" I slapped feebly at his wrist.

"Cheers," he winked. Seriously, what was with the winking?

"What's it going to take, then?" I asked, watching his face for a sign of what he might say. "What's it going to take for you to come over to the dark side?" I gestured at myself.

He smiled. He reached into his breast pocket again. I half-expected him to produce a tiny pad of paper and a ballpoint pen, scribble an obscene amount of money on it, fold it, and pass it to me. Instead, he slid his phone across the table.

"My children — all children, *God's children* — are very important to me."

I looked down at the photo of the cherub children. I should have known what the senator was getting at, but I didn't quite get it yet. Instead, I just nodded dumbly.

"I love kids," I mumbled. I skewered an olive, suddenly starving. Juice spurted out when I bit into it.

"I knew you'd see things my way," he said.

What? Senator Montgomery patted my arm. He poked his own toothpick into my second olive and I thought he was going to eat it. But he didn't. Instead, he fed it to me. I saw the olive coming and recoiled. *This is how he thinks it's going to go, then,* I thought. *He's going to feed me whatever he wants to feed me, and I just have to eat it?* I wanted to slap his hand, for real this time, and pour my drink on him. I was repulsed, but I leaned forward and allowed him to place the olive on my tongue. I chewed it up as inelegantly as possible.

"I'm not sure I follow you, sir," I said, but I was beginning to follow him. I flashed on a memory of Lorelai promoting her book, *No Voice of Their Own: Protecting the Future of America's Pre-Born.*

Damn. He wanted me to reverse course on reproductive freedom. He wanted my promise to go soft on crisis pregnancy centers and "heartbeat" laws and whatever else the right wing had up their grimy sleeves. Then and only then would he endorse me for the judgeship.

"I think you know what I'm saying," he said. "What I need from you is to say that you love children. *All* children."

I told the senator I wasn't feeling well and excused myself. I gathered my coat to leave. I wouldn't compromise my position on abortion rights — how could I, this was my entire career! I left The Monocle that day feeling not the satisfaction of having denied a misogynist his deepest desire, but rather the uncomfortable heat of a bridge burning behind me.

This time being at the Monacle is different because Frank Francis is different. He isn't a fascist on steroids like his colleague Senator Montgomery, but Libertarians are odd ducks. I always have the impression they're making up shit as they go. I drain my dirty martini, and, his eyebrows raised, Frank follows suit. The waiter appears with another. He hands it to me and I take a thirsty gulp, nearly downing the whole thing as if it could save me. I hadn't met with Frank before because his particular brand of Libertarianism involves never endorsing federal judges. He abstains on all votes for the judiciary. Given this policy and my uncomfortable past with him, I had been more than happy to put him in the "no way" column and move on to earning more viable votes. I feel the liquor flow through me and it seems as if my whole career is flashing before my eyes.

I think of all the women who have sat across from me in the variety of dingy spaces that the Women's Rights Initiative leased before a generous donor gave us the funds for a slick office building with security.

I think of woman after woman who shared with me the most intimate details of their lives and marriages and health.

I think of how much good I could do for women from the federal bench. Suddenly it's as if they're all with me, right here at this table.

"I had an abortion, you know. Once, when I was very young. My boyfriend's mother paid for it."

"I just wasn't ready to be a mother."

"I don't regret it."

"I've always wondered what he or she would have been like, but I know I did the right thing."

"I love my kids, but if I had it to do over again ... I would've waited until I was much older."

I think of the women who left abusive situations thankful they didn't have kids. I think of women who gave birth behind bars.

I think of Elena Morales. I think of the words I read in her statement about Jeff. She wrote that she thought she'd never get over him. Then he got someone else pregnant and just like that, she couldn't be so stupid anymore. Just like that, she had evidence that he was lying when he said he loved her. He'd gone and made a baby with another woman. *A baby*, Elena wrote, *changes everything*.

Those words stick with me because they speak to my truest feelings about choice. To have a choice about anything, a woman needs to be able to have a choice about when she becomes a mother. A woman needs to be able to decide when and if her everything would change. Yet, here I was sitting across from another U.S. Senator who was certainly about to ask me to compromise a belief to advance my career.

The saddest part is that I am actually considering it. Whatever Frank is up to, I wish he would just spit it out so I can think about how far I'm willing to compromise my core values.

I walked into this restaurant twenty minutes ago thinking that I was a woman with unshakeable convictions. I might be willing to compromise for the ability to do right by more people, I tell myself, but in no way would I sell out on my beliefs. I went in thinking that I had a firm grip on who I am. Frank hasn't even opened his mouth yet, and I'm willing to give him what he wants. I'm pitiful.

"I'm sorry, Frank, but I'm not feeling all that well. I think I'd better head home, but you've given me a lot to think about."

"Elaine?" He was looking at me oddly. "I haven't said anything yet." "Right," I say.

"You do look a little tipsy," he says. "Maybe you should have a slice of bread." He lifts the basket toward me.

"I'm just a bit lightheaded," I tell him, gathering my purse. I open it up, stare uselessly inside. "Tell me something, Frank. Why did you call me? You don't vote on the judiciary, so—"

"I heard you were nominated," he says. "But that's not why we're here. I have a little problem. I need representation. Of the very discreet variety." He looks pointedly at me and I know what he means, and that he also knows someone has told me about his underground life. "A mediation, a private agreement."

"You need an intermediary," I say. *To pay someone hush money,* I don't add. "Listen, I don't normally do that kind of thing."

"And I don't normally vote on judgeships."

Great. He wants me to be his bag man.

He lets the silence hang over our table. He leans

back, appraising me. He waits.

Someone once told me that the person at the table who says the least is always the one with the most power. So I reach silently for my martini, resolved to remain quiet until he says something useful. I lift the martini to my lips, crossing my legs coolly, and my knee catches the edge of the table, jostling my elbow. Dirty vodka sloshes into my lap, pooling in a sickly green puddle on my periwinkle pencil skirt.

Frank reaches for a heavy cloth napkin and begins dabbing at my thighs. I snatch the napkin from him and swat at his hands.

"I've got it," I snap.

"You sure do," he says, his smirk infuriating.

"You win, Frank," I say. I look around for the waiter, and again onto my damp lap. The martini that should currently be sliding down my throat is now soaked into my clothing. "I'll represent you. What do you need? Who did you fuck over this time?"

The smirk leaves his lips. "No need for incivility," he says.

Why, whenever you challenge a man on his shitty behavior, does he chastise you for not being gentler about it?

"I have a headache," I tell him. "Just spit it out."

"It's for my nephew," he says. "Kid's a guard out at the medium-security facility in Bethesda. Some kind of disciplinary thing, a scuffle with an inmate that got out of hand. She's filed a complaint."

What is it with prison guards I think, as the waiter finally appears, taking care of the spill with perfect discretion and snapping his fingers at the busboy to fetch a replacement.

"My nephew's no boy scout," Frank says, "but he sure as hell didn't assault anybody. I've known him all his life.

"So how did a little scuffle turn into assault," I ask.

"The prisoner is seriously mentally ill, she shouldn't even be in with the general population."

"And you're going to need her to drop charges and sign an NDA, I suppose?" "Correct."

"And the payoff?"

"Five grand."

Cheap bastard, I think. Just enough to turn a prisoner's head but not enough to make any kind of change in her life, not even enough for a down payment on a house for the kids she'll never see grow up. My martini finally arrives and I gulp at it, not giving a damn about Frank's judgmental grin.

"Is this prisoner actually mentally ill or are you just calling her crazy?" I demand. "Is she competent?" And then with a sickening thud something occurs to me. "What kind of assault are we talking about?"

"Does it matter?" Frank says. "Tell me, how many confirmation votes do you have?"

What an asshole. What an arrogant prick. Of course it matters. He wants me to funnel hush money for a prison rape. I take another healthy sip of my dirty martini, our college days coming back to me in a heady swirl, and all common sense flies from my head. I speak my actual thoughts for a change. "And here I thought you wanted me to pay off some gay porn star."

I regret my words the moment they leave my mouth. Still, I won't soon forget the look of panic on Frank Francis's smug handsome face.

He recovers quickly, leans back in his chair, the color drained from his cheeks. "So it's like that," he says softly.

"Don't play the victim, Frank," I say. "You're lousy at it."

"My private life—"

"Save the hypocrisy," I tell him, finishing my drink in one more gulp. "Just have the details sent to my office. I'll have your damn signature by Monday."

Chapter Nine

I escape the restaurant without being spotted by colleagues or the media, or so I think. However the next morning I wake up to my phone exploding with texts and email notifications, the most recent one from Jules. *WHAT THE FUCK WERE YOU THINKING MEETING WITH HIM, ELAINE? AND EVEN IF THAT WEREN'T THE STUPIDEST THING ON THE FACE OF THE PLANET, WHAT THE ACTUAL FUCK WERE YOU THINKING NOT TELLING ME?*

When Jules breaks out into what she calls 'shouty caps', I know that I'm in for a world of hurt. How did she even know about the meeting?

As I'm making my coffee and avoiding my phone, it strikes me. Oh Lord, no, please don't let it be a gossip rag. Please not that.

The D.C. gossip circuit is famously influential. The gossip rag writer is the bitter opposite to the DC restaurateur's blood oath to keep quiet. While they're no longer the mainstay they were in the heyday of Senators

Francis and Montgomery, and while everyone will tell you that nobody cares about newspapers anymore, and while millennials are even promising us that blogging is dead, the D.C. gossip circuit is alive and well.

Some might say that the advent of the smartphone means that we don't need snoops with notebooks and eyes trained on politicians to capture every stupid thing they say. We just need YouTube and Twitter and, of course, memes.

The people who say this are discounting one very important factor. A gossip blog called *The Other Secret Service*. It's alive and well and anyone who's anyone in the Beltway knows to live in fear of its creator. She goes by the alias Mrs. Anna Strong – named after a female member of the Culper Ring, a network of American Revolutionary spies. Her namesake is said to have hung a black petticoat on her clothesline to signal the availability of new military intelligence to ship-running spies on the Long Island Sound.

No one knows for sure who today's Anna Strong is, but many D.C. insiders have their suspicions. Her profile picture is the disembodied lower-half of a woman in a short black petticoat. She wears one blood red pump and one electric blue pump, and her legs go on for days. Every so often a 'mystery solved' tweet will surface from somebody hoping to expose her, featuring a side-by-side comparison of Mrs. Anna Strong's leggy avatar and a press photograph cropped to show only the mile-long gams of a female senator, a high-powered lobbyist or a congressman's wife.

I scroll through the rest of my notifications. Seventeen texts from numbers I don't recognize, but I suspect that they might be Ted's. Kendall. Kendall. Jules. Jules. Jules. Jules.

I don't have it in me to read Ted's texts and I already know Jules is pissed, so I open Kendall's.

Mom, call me.

Seriously, Mom, now.

I know it's horrible, but I can't bring myself to call her. There was a time when I responded to every output from my daughter. A time when she'd scream and I'd come running with my blouse half open. But I can't give her what she needs right now. I don't even *know* what she needs.

Whatever happened, whatever Jules is shouty capping about, it's bad. I open my email inbox. I'd cleared it out before bed, but now I have 75 new messages.

I open the most recent from Jules and I find a link: theothersecretservice.net/senate?ref=woman_scorned_the_monocle. I instantly feel prickly and hot. I click the link and stare at the blog

Header — there they are, Mrs. Anna Strong's creamy pale legs contrasting starkly with the black tulle petticoat.

My next thought is absurd and irrational. I know that those legs can't possibly belong to April McFarland. I know that can't be the smooth, glistening skin that Ted allegedly touched without consent. I know it's not her.

But still. Still, I long desperately for a photograph of April McFarland's lower body, so I can rule out the slim possibility. I'm also such a coward that I am tempted to call Jules instead of reading the blog entry for myself. I'm tempted to treat it the way I treated the reviews of my book, *Lady Justice*. "Just put the criticisms in bullet form," I said to her the day the *New York Times* reviewed the book. "No fancy metaphors. Spare me the artful comparisons. Just the facts, ma'am."

But this isn't a book review, it's a gossip column, and the only fact that will matter is this: I went to a restaurant with my college ex-boyfriend, the Libertarian jerkoff Senator Frank Francis, and someone saw us. I don't want to look, but I'm really tired of staring at these perfectly taut cellulite-free legs. I begin to scroll.

The Other Secret Service

a revolutionary fly on the wall

SPOTTED: Litigator's Lady Living it up with Libertarian Lawmaker?

Posted by Mrs. Anna Strong 1/31/17 – 7:03AM

When Mrs. Strong spotted this unlikely pair upstairs at the Monocle, she simply couldn't turn a blind eye, now could she? Whatever is that old saying about a woman scorned? As Mrs. Strong watched this camera-ready pair enjoy dirty martinis, she remembered the adage at last. A woman scorned: it's only a matter of time before she swaps Senators and begins having drinks with a certain philandering elected official on trial in her big-shot litigator hubby's latest case!

Maybe it's a job interview, not a date (yes, dear reader, there is a difference!)? Good thing this force-of-nature is past her child-bearing years, amirite? As for the sharply dressed legislator-in-question, Mrs. Anna Strong has only one thing to say: in his case, justice may very well indeed be a lady.

Posted in: *spotted*

Tagged: *monocle, the | secret | juicy | affair | scandal | congress*

I know it's impossibly petty, and there are a dozen other things to be outraged about in this stupid article, but I'm offended first that she referred to Ted as a bigshot. What am I, chopped liver?

Anna Strong has hit me where it hurts. *I'm the one* who climbed the ladder of professional success with our child strapped to my back. *I'm the one* who managed her existence, outsourcing a task to Ted only when the inconvenience of it exceeded the odds that he would fuck it up. *I'm the one* who was both an attentive mother and an excruciatingly competent attorney and professor.

But Ted? Well, according to Mrs. Anna Strong of *The Other Secret Service,* Ted is the fucking bigshot. Isn't that rich? Isn't that always the way it goes?

And really? It wouldn't have occurred to Anna Strong that I was wooing Frank Francis for his vote and not his dick? How much investigating would it have taken to discover I'm a goddamn judicial nominee? If she weren't such a sexist creep, she might have asked the more interesting question, which was why Elaine Bower Camden was wasting her time lobbying that Libertarian dickwad. She should have wondered what kind of morally repugnant and barely legal deal I was agreeing to in order to land that 60th vote.

I suppose I should be grateful for this woman's internalized misogyny.

Mrs. Anna Strong is too busy looking for a sex scandal

to see what was right under her nose: a judicial nominee making a backroom bargain with a good old boy. I don't know which narrative is worse, the sex scandal or the political scandal. If Jules is right, I may be facing both at the same time.

Seething, I hurl my phone across the carpet. I'm so mad, I sink to the floor and force myself to do that stupid alternate nostril breathing Jules is always going on about. Then I go to the kitchen for some ice cream. I eat it like a starving refugee while staring at the rosebush still sitting there in my kitchen. *Dammit, Ted.*

In the early years of my marriage, I could avoid letting my tender professional pride get hurt. For the most part, working for the Women's Rights Initiative, surrounded by women, not much sexist conflict got in my way in the day-to-day. Of course, the subtle insults would happen, as they do to all women. From time to time, for example, I'd overlap with Ted on a case. We'd sit in a meeting with stakeholders, and everyone would virtually ignore my idea until Ted repeated it.

This infuriating imbalance of power between my husband and me got progressively worse from the time we had Kendall, and it never improved. In the beginning, Ted tried to help, but his attempts were half-hearted. He took a month's worth of paternity leave when I returned to work from my two weeks off. All I heard about from my co-workers on my first day back to work was how great it was that Ted was willing to stay home and 'babysit'. I wanted to scream at colleagues who should have known better: *It's not babysitting when it's your own baby! It's called parenting!*

Besides that, he outsourced his entire paternity leave to his mother. On my maternity leave, I walked endless loops around our first-floor with a sleeping baby and occasionally managed to microwave a Lean Cuisine, take a shower, or pee. On his leave, Ted published four peer-reviewed articles while Vivian rocked Kendall and made us an ungodly amount of freezer food. I was both outraged at his failure to parent our child directly and in admiration of his ability to find the loophole in everything, including paternity leave. Why hadn't I, too, leaned on friends and family for more help? Vivian had been thrilled with the arrangement; it gave her time to bond with her only grandchild.

But I never slowed down my parenting just because I was working. I stayed up all night baking Kendall's preschool class treats or nursing her fever, and was told I seemed distracted at work. Meanwhile, Ted practically got a damn parade for taking her to the park. Despite the fact that my employer was, at the time, quite woman-friendly, I was still 'mommy-tracked', or more accurately, mom-backtracked. I was assigned to work solely on cut-and-dried or hopeless cases. Cases that were allocated less valuable resources like, well, me.

Meanwhile, Ted continued to thrive professionally, entering private litigation. He made partner at his firm when Kendall was three, just around the time people began to hound me about when we were going to give her a sibling. Nobody at work ever asked Ted that, I was almost certain.

I wanted another baby. I did. Often when I didn't knock out cold on the train ride home, I daydreamed of Kendall meeting a baby brother in the hospital. We talked about a second child. Ultimately, Ted left it up to me. Of course, he left it up to me. He left everything complicated up to me. In the end, all I could think about was my life outside the Mommy Hole. It felt like a sinkhole had engulfed my professional life as soon as I'd peed on the test stick.

If anyone had told me that I'd be stuck with the heavy-lifting, I'd have reconsidered parenthood. Not only did I birth a baby and nurse a baby, I often pumped at work. I took her to the dentist, whom she'd promptly bitten hard enough to draw blood. I stocked enough white flour-based foods to keep her from starving to death during her picky phase. Ted read her stories, proudly recorded her kindergarten musical, and took her to museums every other Saturday.

Yesterday Elena Morales said, "Everyone was always saying what a great guy Jeff was for taking on me and my two kids. Yeah? Well, Jeff was a fucking drug dealer and an abuser. Okay?"

Ted is none of those things, of course. He's one of the good ones. Not that it mattered at the time; I hated to be such a cliché, almost as much as I hated that Ted had to be micromanaged. He had to be informed that we needed to maintain a steady supply of juice boxes, string cheese, tear-free shampoo, and baby wipes to keep our lives from descending into the bowels of hell. Shit, Ted hadn't even bought *his own toilet paper* since the early 1990's.

At home, I did the emotional and domestic labor. At the office, I did the kind of eye-gougingly boring work I hadn't been assigned since I was junior counsel. This went on for years.

Then, finally, my baby grew into a school-aged child, and I had enough time to put on concealer and iron my skirts and claw my way toward the top.

I loved Ted, and I loved how much he loved Kendall. I still love Ted. I still love how much he loves Kendall.

It's never been about taking anything away from Ted. It's about getting credit for my work. It's always been about equity.

Back in the bedroom, I ignore my email notifications and open a new message to Jules.

'*Anna Strong is a liar*', I type. But she hadn't exactly lied. More like speculated rampantly. I delete my text.

'*It's not me*', I type, but that's just a blatant untruth. Obviously, it's me.

'*Maybe no one will know it's me*', I type. I send the message.

I know I should call Kendall, but I don't have it in me right now. I can feel myself starting to panic. My phone buzzes. It's another text from Jules. She has sent a photo. It's a screenshot of a tweet from @ MrsAnnaStrong: "#Spotted: Guess who? Get the secret deets on the blog!" Below it there's a picture. It's dark and low-resolution, but I can make out Frank's broad shoulders. My hand rests gently atop his. The paparazzo must have had us focused in his sights, waiting for the moment I reached across the table and touched Frank's wrist to emphasize my point. Did he know this was a habit of mine, a tic? That I touch people when I talk to them? Was he waiting for me to do it? Looking at the photo, I can remember the feel of Frank's crisp blue dress shirt. My fingers are obscured by shadow. The only identifying details are my watch and, nearly out of frame, the hint of my chin and a ruff of my platinum blonde hair.

Maybe it isn't a man who'll wreck my life but a woman who talks about herself in third person! I text Jules back with a series of further invectives about Anna Strong. Then I calm down.

Is there any chance that no one will care about this? I type.

ZERO, she replies. *I mean, Anderson Cooper follows her. GREAT.*

The vultures are putting two and two together.

To duck the subject I'm considering some snarky response about vultures doing math. Thankfully my phone rings, and desperate to end this text conversation with Jules, I pick it up without looking.

"Hello, Elaine, it's Brenda," says the voice of Ted's administrative assistant, her voice characteristically chipper. "I have Ted on the line, may I patch him through?"

Chapter Ten

"**A**re you there, Elaine? Hello," Brenda says. I want to hang up. I want to scream. I think about telling Brenda that I don't want to talk to Ted; I want to kick Ted in the nuts.

"I'm here," I say. "Put him through if you must."

"Elaine," Ted says, and I feel a rush of emotions. I think of my persona in Anna Strong's ridiculous column, the god-awful meeting with Frank Francis, and my reputation being on the line. Because of Ted, I'll either end up ruined for bargaining with Frank or ruined for reversing course on decades of championing women.

Or, somehow, for both.

I'm between a rock and a hard place, and suddenly I just want a soft place to land. I hear Ted's deep voice and think of his arms around me. I also think of him *naked*.

"What do you want," I ask.

"I'm outside our house," he says. "Please let me in."

Damn it.

I walk down the staircase, trying not to think about the walls on either side of it covered in my favorite photographs of our life together. Me sitting on Ted's lap at a holiday party, in a sleek red dress that no longer zips. Ted holding the deliciously chubby apple-cheeked Kendall wearing only her diaper. A large black and white wedding day print of our hands intertwined against the lacy backdrop of my dress. I think again of the weight of his long fingers interlocked with mine and the sweat on his palms. I know right then and there that I'm going to let him in.

Damn it.

Before I open the door, I force myself to think of April McFarland. Does she, too, have a little red dress? Did Ted buy it?

I open the door and it's like I'm seeing Ted for the very first time. He's the sweet puppy-dog-eyed boy I met when I was mousy little Lainey Bower.

In my lifetime of representing women put through the wringer by husbands and boyfriends, I had never truly understood how these women got snowed. Over the years, I had allowed myself to imagine Ted's infidelity or petty crime or whatever, and I had always visualized exactly how I'd respond. I'd open the door or roll down the window. I'd say, "Ted, it's over. I'm putting my foot down." Then I'd slam the door or peel out of the parking lot. I would not be Elena Morales. No way was my own personal Jeff going to screw me over. No. I was smart. I was strong. I wasn't rich, but I was damn close. If I were wronged, I thought, I'd take no bullshit and no prisoners. I am woman!

That's the hypothetical reaction I've always imagined for myself. What I actually do is quite different.

First, I begin to cry. The gulf between us closes instantly. I am in his arms before I know it. I can smell his skin and his Old Spice deodorant. It is familiar, both comforting and exciting. Against my wet cheek, I can feel the crisp cotton poplin of the shirt I bought him. Then, I'm undoing its buttons. He takes my face in his hands and wipes my tears and kisses me. I wrap my arms around him, and his hands make their way down my body. I slip my shirt off and he slides down my pajama bottoms.

We don't even close the front door. Instead, we sink to the floor of the foyer, desperate for each other. I'm on my back on the cold tile and then he's on top of me. The weight of him is so deliciously reassuring. The feel of his skin on mine makes me feel, for a moment, like nothing else matters.

"Is this okay," Ted asks. "Does this feel good?"

Relief floods through my entire body. These words are as familiar as my name. I can't count the number of times he's said this to me in the course of our decades together. How could I have ever thought that my gentle husband could have hurt a woman? Even in the midst of the most desperate and frantic lovemaking, here he was seeking my enthusiastic approval.

"Yes," I say, and I mean it. "Please."

He held me the same way he always has and I let him, the same way I always have.

Afterward we lie on the floor in the foyer naked and sweating. Our silence is deafening. From the combination of crying and my mild hangover, I feel overcome with exhaustion. Normally, sex with Ted amps me up. He's always fallen asleep after. I've always loved to snuggle into his warm body for a few minutes and then step out of bed energized. I've always loved puttering around the house to the symphony of his mild snores.

I miss those moments.

Right now, I just want to play Ted's role. I want to climb under the covers and fall into a deep, contented sleep. We lie on the floor holding hands but not speaking. I stand up, tug his hand. I motion for him to follow me. He does. I lead him to the bedroom. I turn down the sheets, lie down, and pat the bed beside me. He spoons me and I feel my eyes well up with tears again. I really thought this part of us was over. I thought I had lost him. I thought that every tender thing between us had been a lie. I thought my heart was hard and closed to him, but look at us now: falling asleep together in our own bed.

Ted's breathing becomes deep and heavy, his arm around me, a dead sleeping weight. The last time we had sex in the middle of the day and lay in bed letting the afternoon fade into evening, it had been the end of a months-long dry spell. Ted was in the thick of preparing for the suit against Senator Montgomery. I was still angry that he'd taken it on. I'd been trying to convince him to put one of his up-and-coming young litigators on the case. "*Let someone else make a name for themselves,*" I said, "*don't take on all this stress at this stage in your career.*" What I had meant was: '*Don't attach your name to this*'. What I'd really meant was: '*Don't attach my name to this*'.

The following day, Ted had hired April McFarland to handle the Montgomery case. She'd take the burden of the work and, notably, the responsibility if they lost; Ted would stay in the background and mentor her through it. He'd been so thrilled about taking my advice.

"I have some good news," he said when he called me at the office the following afternoon. "I think you're going to be really proud of me." I thought he was going to tell me he'd dropped the case or, at the very least, that he'd given it to Nathan Meyers. Instead he told me he'd taken on a protegee. Young and pretty lawyer, April McFarland. All this time I've alternated between blaming him and feeling guilty for blaming her, but the irony is that hiring her was *my* idea.

Ted is now full-on snoring. My phone battery has long since died, and I haven't bothered to plug it in. Jules is going to kill me. God only knows what vultures have seized on @mrsannastrong's Twitter. I hope they haven't contacted Senator Francis for comment. God only knows what he'd say.

Damn it.

All chances of being able to sleep now are shot to hell. I sit up and turn on the light. I deliberately make as much noise as possible while searching for my phone and plugging it in. I open and close the night stand and purposely drop the remote on the floor.

Turns out, I still know the exact combination of noises needed to wake up my husband. Next to me, he stirs. He groans. He opens his eyes and shields them from the light.

"What the hell are you doing over there," he mumbles.

"Hi." I say this in the same tone in which I'd say *shut the hell up, jackass.*

My tone apparently escapes his notice. "Hi," he says. He smiles. I know that look. He wants me to get back under the covers. Hell, he probably wants me to dive under the covers and go straight for his penis. Of course he does. "How're you doing, baby?" "I'm not sure," I say. "Honestly, Ted, until I figure it all out I would appreciate if you did not call me baby."

"Understandable," he says, and to his credit, doesn't roll his eyes. He knows I'm mad! I have him right where I want him.

"I'm so angry," I tell him, my lip quivering. "I'm glad you're here. But I also want to kill you."

"I get it," he says. "But where would you hide my body?" He winks. It reminds me of Frank Francis. Do they take a class on winking? I don't even think I *can* wink.

"We have to talk about this," I say. "I don't want to talk about this, but we have to."

"Honey, I've been trying to talk to you since the beginning. You're the one who didn't want to talk."

This enrages me. I can feel my blood boiling. He

changed his fucking phone number!

"Don't put this on me," I huff. I get up and walk into the closet.

"Where are you going? You're seriously just going to walk away?" Ted taunts.

"I'll go wherever I want!" I yell. I open the drawer and all my damn pajamas are gone. In the hamper. Of course they are! I grab my fluffy lavender robe from the hook.

"Relax, I was just ... cold." *I wish I felt cold towards him,* I think. "I'm not walking away," I say, emerging from the closet. "You *wish* I were walking away."

"So, let's talk," he says. "Let's talk."

"Okay, you're the one who has the explaining to do," I say. "Tell me what in the hell is happening."

"What do you want to know?"

"Don't be obtuse. And quit with the jokes. I want to know everything," I say. "But mostly I want to know if you slept with her, Ted. I'm serious. I want to know. Did you?" I can't bear to look at him, so I look at the floor, where I've spent so much time lately. Women often tell me that they have trouble getting out of bed. Me, I have trouble getting off the floor. It's as if I want to find the lowest physical point to match my mental state.

"You deserve the truth," he says. He scoots over to

my side of the bed and sits next to me. He puts his arm around me, and I'm too scared of what he's about to say to fight his touch.

"The truth," my husband says, "is that I wanted to. The truth is that I thought about it constantly, from the moment she came in for her interview. I wanted to know what it would be like to be with her. It had been so long since we …"

"You asshole," I say. "You asshole. Don't touch me." But I make no move to shrug out of his grip or take his hands off me. Instead I sink further into him.

"But I didn't, Elaine, I swear to god, I didn't."

"Why …"

"Because I love you. Because I love you so much and I would never do that to you."

"No, I'm not asking why you didn't sleep with her, Ted. I'm asking why I should believe you! Why in the hell should I believe you? Tell me."

"Because it's true."

"Oh, come on," I say, remembering Mrs. Anna Strong's column. "You're a 'bigshot' litigator. You can do better than that." He hates air quotes, so I make them just to piss him off.

"Look, you're the only one who can decide what to believe. My job isn't to convince you; it's to be honest with you. I wanted to sleep with her. She's a beautiful young woman. She even reminds me a little of you."

"Oh, buddy," I say, feeling my blood pressure go through the roof. "Of all the things in all the world to say, you have found the absolute stupidest one. Congratulations!"

"It may be stupid, but it's true. I missed you, and I was spending so much time with her. I just sort of fell for her. I just got a little crush on her and she knew it."

"No," I yell. "No, Ted! It wasn't a crush. You didn't get a crush on her. You harassed her. Or worse. You assaulted her!"

"Elaine," he yelps. He's wounded. "I never thought that you'd believe that.

His eyes are watering. "I just never thought that you'd believe that."

He stands up, turns, and stomps down the hall. I curl in a ball on the floor again and sob. I listen to him in the foyer ruffling through the clothes we'd so carelessly ripped off.

I can't stand the thought of him leaving. I leap up from the carpet and run down the hall. "Where the hell do you think you're going?" I yell.

"I'm not going anywhere," he says. "I have to show you something."

He hands me a piece of paper folded in half. I open it to reveal a photograph of two women at a baby shower, grinning happily at the camera, arms intertwined as though sisters, or best friends. On the right was a smiling, glowing April McFarland, younger than today. On the left, in a floral maternity dress, is a woman I can't quite place. Something about her looks familiar. Does she work for Ted, too? I study her stiff pageant hairstyle and caked on makeup. So much bronzer.

Then it hits me. All that's missing is four impish blond kids.

There is April McFarland with her delicate manicured hands, gently cupping the third Mrs. Montgomery's first baby bump.

"They're friends?" I gasp. "April McFarland and Lorelei Montgomery?"

"I've been fucked by my protegee," he says, miserably.

"Be careful what you wish for," I almost reply. But I don't. This time, I keep my big mouth shut.

Chapter Eleven

Who would have ever thought that a photo of the pregnant belly of Lorelai Montgomery would save my marriage? Life is so strange. After Ted showed me the picture, my first impulse was to think it was doctored. *Well, clearly this is photoshopped*, I thought. But then I remembered that Ted has the technological skills of a muskrat wearing a blindfold. I guess he could have paid someone to fix the photo, but it sure *looks* real.

Besides, what a strange lie that would be! If there's one thing I've learned over the years it's that, when people lie, they usually start small and then the lie gets bigger and bigger. Most people don't *begin* with something outlandish.

Furthermore, Ted is a horrible liar. Horrible.

If that weren't enough, there was also the way he'd looked at me when I'd accused him of assaulting April. The pain in his crisp blue eyes. The edge to his voice. The tear sliding down his stubbly cheek.

Still, I keep looking at the photo, closing my eyes and then opening them, as if trying to refresh my vision. I don't trust what I'm seeing. Why do I always have to be so incredibly skeptical? Finally, I let myself believe it. I let the photo become proof of an elaborate setup, a plot to destroy my husband, and I feel relief rush through my entire body. I once read somewhere that relief is an aphrodisiac. It's true. I am so relieved, in fact, that I practically climb on top of Ted.

We leave the picture lying on the coffee table and retreat once again to the bedroom. The photo ignited the tiny spark of faith I still had in my husband. The betrayal of his admission that he'd *wanted* to sleep with April McFarland stunned me, sure, but that was *normal*. We've been married for multiple decades. Of course his eye had wandered. Of course a beautiful young woman who paid attention to him and likely stroked his ego had gotten his attention.

Of course he was tempted. But Ted is no sexual predator. He's my husband.

My adorable, loyal, albeit easily distracted, sheepdog of a husband. For days, my heart has burned with anger. Now, it burns again for Ted.

Again.

He's next to me snoring softly. I feel such relief that,

if he's being honest like I think he is, April McFarland has never heard this sound. She has never felt the weight of him on top of her. She has never touched his soft belly or wrapped her legs around his waist.

I believe him. I do.

I think.

But why did April lie?

What on earth motivates a woman to say she's been raped if she hasn't?

I've spent my career arguing time and again that women simply do not lie about sexual assault. They just don't. I've said it again and again and again and I believe it. I believe women. I have always said that this unflinching belief in women is the thing that most contradicts my ability to practice the law. We're supposed to treat the law like it's paramount. Like everyone is innocent until proven guilty.

But sexual assault confuses that. Deep down I think, "I don't care what the law says! If a woman tells me a man hurt her, well, I think he did it! He's guilty period!"

In the aftermath of the tape revealing the President bragging about sexual assault, I did a few guest spots on CNN. Women had started coming out of the woodwork accusing him of sexual harassment and assault. Over and over, the President denied it, demanded an apology, and even threatened to sue the media outlets that had run with the stories. That was what the news shows invited me to discuss. Did these women have a case?

But the conversation often changed trajectories and I found myself discussing the concept of false allegations.

"False allegations of assault are very, very rare. Statistically negligible," I'd tell the cameras. I'd insist that women just don't lie about these things. I'd point out over and over again how hard it is to come forward and talk about this kind of abuse. I'd point out that everyone from the news media to their accusers and sometimes even family and friends do whatever it takes to try and silence the accusers.

In my entire career, I've only ever seen two false rape allegations. Back in my public defender days, I'd defended a 17-year-old boy caught in a compromising position with a cognitively impaired classmate. The classmate's mother had walked in on them on the girl's bedroom floor. Shocked, she yelled, "get off her!"

The girl would later admit that she'd been embarrassed by the way she felt about the boy. She'd been mortified by the fact that her mother had seen the boy's bare bottom. She'd been ashamed that she'd 'done that' with a boy she wasn't married to. She thought that her mother thinking that the boy had taken advantage of her was easier than having a conversation about sex.

The story was so very sad. I felt so bad for the girl, who was so young and so uninformed. Later, she said she cared about the boy and *wanted* to have sex with him. I felt so bad for the boy, who had told the court over and over that he loved the girl. He said that he loved her smile and loved the flowers she doodled in her notebook in the remedial math class they shared. He said that he loved the mixtape she had made him.

I even felt sorry for the mother. The mother who was so dog tired from advocating for her daughter's educational needs, worrying about her not making friends, or being excluded, that she couldn't see how *normal* her kid was, what a typical teenager she was.

Somewhere I still have a copy of the letter the girl wrote to her mother exonerating the boy. She wrote it on the wide-ruled paper they give to elementary school children to practice their handwriting. 'I think I love him, mama', the letter said. 'I wanted to do that'.

The second case is the one that came immediately to mind when I saw the photo of April and Lorelai. Years ago, I worked on a complicated case: the co-owner of a chain of hotels had had a dispute with his business partner. He then went home and knocked his wife around until she agreed to falsely accuse his partner of rape.

Is that what's going on here? Is April being intimidated by the senator? If so, why?

It's easy to see why a woman would lie to keep a husband from beating her.

It's easy to see why someone like Elena Morales would agree to keep some packages for a low life like Jeff.

There are always connections. Motivations. But why April? What do they have on her?

My head begins to swirl with the millions of ways that April and Lorelai might know each other. Had they been college roommates? Sorority sisters? Are they cousins? Did Senator Montgomery have an affair with April and threaten to tell his wife unless she did this for him?

Did what for him? Seduce my husband? But why?

It all seems so far-fetched that it's easier to conclude that Ted is lying. But that picture.

That picture.

I leave Ted snoring beside me and tiptoe out of the room to look at it again. I put on my cheater glasses and hold it up to the light. I'm so tempted to draw a mustache on April McFarland's face. I'd like to vandalize her perfectly dewy skin and black out one of her flawless teeth. Maybe even draw some horns emerging from the massive pile of waves on her head.

I imagine April and Lorelai on a girls' shopping trip at Nordstrom's in Chevy Chase, purchasing gobs of size double-zero clothing with Senator Montgomery's credit card. It's easy to imagine them side-by-side at an expensive make-up counter complimenting one another's elaborate eyeshadow. All I have to do is squint and I can see April planning the shower for Lorelei's 'miracle' baby.

Kendall would say they look like The Plastics from *Mean Girls*, one of her favorite movies. She loves it so much that I've seen it a million times, too. I imagine Lorelei as Gretchen, the dumb but self-righteous sidekick. April is Regina, the queen bee. Or maybe it's the other way around.

It's all speculation. But the truth is out there somewhere and I'm going to find it.

It turns out that the truth may very well be sitting in Ted's room at the Hay-Adams hotel, where he told me he'd been holed up since the news broke.

When he wakes up and finds me staring at the photo, he starts to tell me how he's spent the past days trying to figure out what happened and why. "I've basically made a war room," he says, sleepily.

"That's my husband," I say, nuzzling into his chest.

Ever the legal brain, he's built a complete case analysis file on April McFarland. He says that he has all her background check files. The content of her social media accounts. Her employment history. Even her credit report.

"I have printouts of every text and email we've ever exchanged," he says.

My heart sinks at the idea. Will there be proof of their emotional intimacy? Flirting? Compliments? Communiques that walk a fine line? I can't allow myself to think about it. The sting of Ted's admission that he had a crush on April McFarland is too sharp. Too fresh.

Besides that, the idea of all that information sitting in a hotel room makes hairs of paranoia shoot up the back of my neck. Suddenly it seems so naïve of Ted to have left all those clues unattended.

"Oh my god, Ted," I shriek. "You have to go get that stuff and bring it back here! What if someone manages to get in there? What if housekeeping starts snooping or something? What if Montgomery hired some kind of …"

"Some kind of what?"

"I don't know … a goon or something?"

"What is this? *The Godfather?*"

"Look," I say, "I wouldn't put anything past Jimmy

Montgomery. I had dinner with that smarmy slimeball and he told me that he'd vote for my confirmation if I renounced my pro-choice views, so ..."

"Wait, what? You ..."

"We don't have time for this right now," I say, leaping out of bed and fetching Ted's clothes. "You've got to get over there and get that stuff."

"What time is it?"

"Three."

"AM or PM?"

"PM."

"Oh my god," he says. "Okay, I'll go get it. And I'll pick us up some takeout." "You read my mind," I say, my stomach growling.

He gets dressed and heads out. After he's gone, I run a steaming hot shower. For the first time in days, I don't start crying as soon as I step in. I do, however, feel a buzz of anxiety. I feel like I'm being watched or something. Jumpy and uneasy. That's perhaps my least favorite part of this situation: how paranoid it has made me.

Normally, the shower is where I have emotional or intellectual breakthroughs, but today it's just nice to let my mind go blank. I breathe in the steam and wash my hair with mint shampoo and apply a deep conditioner and exfoliate. It's a load off my mind to do something simple and frivolous.

By the time I step out of the shower and wrap the towel around my head, I feel clean and renewed. I wipe the steam from the mirror. Staring at my reflection, I see that my skin is red from the heat and the lingering post-coital flush. I've gotten used to not recognizing the woman staring back at me. But this time, I know exactly who I am.

April McFarland made me doubt my husband. She made me doubt all of my convictions. I could forgive that. But what I can't forgive is how much harder she has made it for the women who really have been assaulted to come forward. She's fed into a long and storied history of women being called liars and whores.

Nope, I can't forgive that.

I'm Elaine Bower Camden, and I'm out for blood.

Chapter Twelve

If someone had told me a day ago that I'd be here right now, I'd have laughed so hard I would have peed in my pants. I'd have looked at that person like they had three heads. But here I am, lying on the couch in my bathrobe willing Ted to return with file boxes full of clues and takeout from our favorite Indian place.

Here I am holding the now-creased photograph of April McFarland and Lorelai Montgomery. I've assembled the evidence that I have in my possession: the picture, the card from the flowers Ted sent with the vase of now desiccated roses, a print out of the calendar reminder for my meeting with Senator Montgomery, and, of course, that god-awful column from Mrs. Anna Strong. Reading it over again, I cringe. *It's a damn good thing my husband is a " big-shot litigator,"* I think. *It might just save our asses.*

Irritated, I huff into my office to retrieve my laptop. I open it and navigate to The Other Secret Service.

For some strange reason, I think that if I can find

out who Mrs. Anna Strong really is, everything will be fine. I click on her profile picture and save it to my downloads. I know there's some fancy way to Google a reverse image search. This is the kind of thing I'd normally ask Jules to do, but I don't even want to look at my phone right now. I think of calling Kendall, but I'm so emotionally exhausted. There's just so much to explain. Where would I even begin?

I have a fleeting thought that maybe all of this — the sex, the picture, the war room — is some elaborate scheme Ted has concocted to get even with me for not believing him. I know in my heart and feel in my bones that it's not.

The image of April McFarland fills my mind and I find myself directing toward her all that anger I felt for Ted. I'd tried so hard to give her the benefit of the doubt, and now I'm just mad. I feel mad for every woman who won't be believed because someone like April lied. I feel mad that, because of her, I've neglected my daughter and my clients. I feel mad that, because of her, my future as a judge is on the line.

But what if she's not actually in on it, I ask myself, once again feeling uncertain. *But she has to be in on this, right? It's way too much of a coincidence for her to know the wife of Jimmy Montgomery.*

I hate being so uncertain. I hate being so wishy-washy. I hate it and I hate her.

My phone buzzes, jarring me out of my thoughts. It's Ted wanting to know if I want the usual. I do. I text back, *Yes, and extra naan!!* I may very well survive all of this, but I'm definitely going to weigh four hundred pounds if I do.

Now that the phone is in my hand, I scroll through the messages from Jules and, of course, they're increasingly more panicked. But I don't see any that say '*That's it, I'm done Elaine. I quit*', so that's a good sign. I text her back '*I'm sorry! I'm so sorry. New development. Can you meet me tomorrow afternoon*'?

I decide to brew a pot of coffee. Again, I walk by the flowers, and I remember how mad they made me. I decide to get rid of them. But I find a pair of scissors and clip one of the roses. For posterity, I think, as if I'll ever want a reminder of this awful time.

The scent of coffee fills the kitchen, and I pour myself a cup. It's rich and luxurious, and the hot liquid warms my belly. I sit down at the computer and open it. I refresh the Google image search on Mrs. Anna Strong, and I stare at the disembodied lower-half of a woman in a short black petticoat. She wears one blood red pump and one blue pump, and her legs go on for even longer than the last time I saw them. I have the same pair of shoes — Pigalle leather Christian Louboutins — but mine aren't fashionably mismatched and instead are a sensible black and, damn, they hurt my feet and I only wear them to court.

"Well, whoever she is, she can afford $485 shoes," I think, remembering the first time I could treat myself to something so absurd and luxurious. I have always gotten such a high from being able to spend my own money on something nice.

I stare at Mrs. Anna Strong's perfectly smooth, shiny gams until they go blurry. Then, I go on a hunt for my damn cheater glasses. For Christmas Ted had put a jeweled glasses chain in my stocking. I'd hated it and refused to wear it. Too old lady. Too school marmish. I'd trashed it and told him I lost it, but I curse myself for that every time I have to hold something two feet from my face. Damn vanity!

I find my glasses on the coffee table next to the photo of April McFarland. I put the readers on and pick up the photograph and bring it back to my desk. The first three image search results lead me back to various 'mystery solved' tweets. One features a side-by-side comparison of the profile and a press photograph cropped to show only the shoes of the junior senator from Colorado. There's another of the mile-long legs of Britt Ashley, an Aetna lobbyist . Another Tweet claiming that Mrs. Anna Strong is actually former First Daughter Jenna Bush. The fourth search result leads me back to the latest post on *The Other Secret Service.* This was leading me nowhere.

My stomach tightens from the coffee and from the anger. I decide not to read the post again, but I really want to. In fact, I want to print it out, mark it up, give it to Mrs. Anna Strong, and tell her to stick it where the sun don't shine.

Instead, I return to the Google image search. There's nothing good there. I sigh — yet another dramatic sigh. Yet again I feel the insatiable urge to google April McFarland.

"What the hell," I say aloud, to nobody. I type her name in the search bar and hit Enter and, suddenly, there's April McFarland's entire life in front of me. There's her social media profiles and her LinkedIn. *Do not write an endorsement, Elaine,* I think, *do not write an endorsement. Don't do it.*

Before I know it, I'm scrolling through the thousands of photographs on her Instagram. She's one of those people who take pictures of their food. I hear Ted's voice in my head. *I wanted to sleep with her. She's a beautiful young woman. She even reminds me a little of you.*

"Seriously, Ted," I say to myself. "I would *never* photograph my salmon."

My stomach growls. I'm so hungry and so irritated with Ted that I begin scrolling furiously.

My phone buzzes. It's Jules. I pick up.

"Finally!" she yells. "Jesus Christ, Elaine!"

The idea that I'm paying someone to talk to me this way suddenly strikes me as hilarious. Between the caffeine and the adrenaline, I feel a little punch drunk. I can't help it and I laugh. I laugh and laugh and laugh.

"What's so funny?" Jules shrieks.

My laughter dies down. "Oh, just my life," I say. "Just my utterly fucked up life."

"I'm glad you're maintaining your sense of humor," she says. "But this is a mess, Elaine."

"Quite the shitshow," I agree.

"Since when do you use that word?"

"I started sometime after my life became a shitshow."

The doorbell rings. It's Ted. *I have a husband who rings the doorbell now. That's just great.*

"I have to go, Jules," I say. "But can you do tomorrow?"

"Elaine! Seriously, you go MIA for …."

"I know," I tell her. "I'm sorry. I'll explain tomorrow."

"Okay, but …."

"Oh, and Jules?"

"Yes?"

"April McFarland is a mole."

"Oh yeah, she's a total weasel."

"No, a mole-mole. A plant."

The doorbell rings again. "I'll explain tomorrow," I say and hang up, cutting Jules off mid-sentence. She's going to kill me.

"Just come in already," I yell to Ted. "It's your own damn house!"

"I know, but it's locked," he yells. I feel a pang of relief. He knows it's still his house. I look back at the laptop, suddenly embarrassed at my snooping. I'm about to slam it shut to hide the evidence and then it occurs to me that I should clear my browser history, but I guess we're past that.

I open the door and there's Ted. Ted who, much to my chagrin, *never* makes two trips to carry anything. He's holding two large file boxes stacked on top of each other. Perched at the top our chicken tikka masala is balanced precariously.

I shake my head and roll my eyes and rescue the takeout bags from the top of the pile.

"It's all there," I say, "is there more in the car?"

"One more box," he says, "But I dropped it outside."

Of course, he did.

"Go get it," I say, "I'm not dressed."

"I see that," he says, reddening. I laugh and open my robe, playfully flashing him.

"Go get it!"

I take out plates and serve up the steaming takeout, and just the smell of the spices makes my mouth water. I can't decide whether I'm more eager to dig into the files or the food, so I decide to do both at once. I carry everything to the table.

Ted returns holding a sheaf of papers and the box.

We begin to shovel the food in, him eating like his food is going to run away as he always does. Me, greedily, as if I have not been eating everything in sight for weeks. Oh, well. There's time for diets when my life isn't falling apart.

Ted spills his water, and I leap up, grabbing the pile of stray documents to save it. Ted runs for the paper towels. I'm tempted to scold him. Instead, I look down at the paper I'm holding. It's a printout of some text messages from April. A single sentence leaps out at me.

'Oh, please, why would a big-shot litigator like you be intimidated by little ol' me'.

Ted sees the look on my face.

"Oh, god," he says. "Oh, god, I'm so sorry."

"I'm not mad," I say. I grab two slices of naan and walk into the living room to find Mrs. Anna Strong's column. Ted follows me.

"Can't we just talk about …"

"I said I'm not mad." I thrust the article at him, "look at this!"

"What does this have to do with …" Then his eyes widen. I can practically see the lightbulb go off in his head. "Big-shot litigator … wait a minute…"

"Exactly!" I shout. "Exactly!"

"Are you saying that she's behind …"

"I mean what are the odds that two people would use that exact phrase?

With the hyphen?"

Excitedly I scoop up my laptop and take it back into the kitchen. Ted is right behind me with the two pieces of paper in his hands.

"I think I need a drink," I say.

"Dear god, I have never needed a drink more," he says. He opens the freezer where we keep the good vodka. "We're out of limes," I say. "And there's no soda."

"Fuck it," Ted says, filling two glasses to the brim. I sip mine, recoiling at the sense memory of my dinner with Senator Francis. In all the hubbub, I'd nearly forgotten about the deal I made with this particular devil and the conversation I would need to have with the prisoner his nephew assaulted. I've been in denial about all of it.

"Seriously," I say, "if ever there were a time for straight vodka, this is it. I feel like I'm in the Twilight Zone."

"Me, too," Ted says, humming the theme song.

I open my laptop. The embarrassment I felt at snooping has faded, and I let Ted look over my shoulder. I scroll through April's Instagram, looking for what? A photo of her plotting my husband's demise? A snapshot of a note that says I'm going to ruin your life Ted Camden?

I don't know what I'm looking for, but I keep scrolling as if I'm on a mission. I sift through shots of April in beanie and scarf, April and a Christmas tree, April posing for a selfie with her dog.

With each passing photo, I feel sicker and angrier and, frankly, drunker. I feel myself cursing under my breath at how pointless this is. How weird this is.

Then I see it, another photo that will change everything.

It's a snapshot of April McFarland's ankles and feet against the backdrop of a dingy subway grate. A photograph staged explicitly to show off a pair of electric blue 4-inch Pigalle leather Christian Louboutin pumps.

Gotcha, bitch, I whisper.

I look up to see Ted's shocked expression.

"What? I said that out loud?" I ask.

"Did I just hear the word *bitch* come out of your mouth?"

We've had this conversation before. Ted says I'm supposed to accept the contemporary usage of *bitch* as some kind of empowered sisterhood thing, but I just can't get past the word as a misogynist slur and have never been able to toss it around.

"Sometimes it's the only word that will do," I say at my screen.

Ted is silent, and when I look up he's frowning at his phone. "It's my mother," he says.

"Don't pick up!" I have to stop myself from shrieking it.

Gently he places the phone face down on the countertop, where it vibrates at us.

"Don't worry," he says. "I won't. But speaking of Vivian. Did you…?"

"Did I call her?" I say. "Have we spoken, since all of this began?"

"Please tell me you didn't," he says.

I lean over the counter and kiss him, hard. "Don't worry," I say. "I haven't."

"But we need to," he says.

"No question that we need to," I reply, flooded with relief that it would be *We* facing Vivian and not just *Me*.

"She needs to hear from us," he agreed.

"Well sure," I say, realizing suddenly the astonishing resources that the retired Congressmember Vivian Harper Camden could bring to this situation. "But more importantly, we need to hear from *her*."

Chapter Thirteen

In the morning, Ted and I get dressed for work as if everything is normal. He's going to his office and I'm going to mine, and in the afternoon we'll meet to strategize with Jules about April McFarland. Ted insists on being there for this meeting. Jules is not going to love that idea.

Ted wants to drive into the city, but I want to take the train. I love the train. I love disappearing into the crowd. I love fantasizing about staying in my seat long after my stop. Then switching to an Amtrak and ending up someplace I've never been before. Far away from the bubble of this city, the bubble of concentrated power and corruption with intellectuals trying to pretend that they aren't steeped in either.

Ted and I walk to the station, holding hands. His strides are long and I have to step quickly to keep up with him. I'm wearing heels, a charcoal pencil skirt, and a pristine ivory blouse I usually save for court dates. My new Burberry plaid trench coat is a little tighter around the middle than it was when I bought it last month. Still, I'm enjoying the prickle of the coming winter in the air.

"So what do you think she wants?" I ask Ted.

"Who?"

"April, you goof," I say. Who else could I possibly be talking about?

He looks puzzled. "I honestly don't know. I've been wracking my brain."

"Maybe it's just money?"

"Sure, money makes sense. It's just that the things she's saying about me, they feel so …"

"Personal," I ask.

"Exactly."

He's right. It all feels personal. It feels like she's invested in taking us down. I guess these things always feel personal. How could they not?

I feel tears start to form in my eyes. Instead of thinking about Ted's betrayal, I focus on the pain in my feet, which isn't difficult because they already hurt like hell. My own Louboutins, tasteful and black, are killing my toe beds. I step over a grate and think of April McFarland again. She won't go away. I swear, if I saw her, I'd wring her neck.

It's early enough to get a seat on the train. I sit next to Ted, pretending this is just a normal commute. He rests his hand on my leg, and I think of how we must look to the other commuters. We must look comfortable, in love.

"It's weird to be on the train together, huh," Ted says.

"It's weird to be *together,*" I say.

He laughs.

I put my earphones in. 'Congratulations' from the musical *Hamilton* blares through my earphones. It's hard not to belt out the lyrics and dedicate them to Ted.

Congratulations

You have invented a new kind of stupid

A 'damage you can never undo' kind of stupid

An 'open all the cages in the zoo' kind of stupid

'Truly, you didn't think this through' kind of stupid.

I hope Ted's juvenile feelings for April McFarland isn't 'damage you can never undo' kind of stupid, but it definitely seems to be 'open all the cages at the zoo' kind of stupid. Kendall introduced me to *Hamilton,* and I'm particularly fond of Angelica Hamilton's invectives against her husband, Alexander, after his affair.

To clear his name about possible financial abuse, Hamilton confessed his dalliance in a published pamphlet. I know exactly how much this must have humiliated his wife.

In my handbag, I'm carrying three photographs: the

snapshot of Lorelai Montgomery and April McFarland, Mrs. Anna Strong's profile pic, and the image from April's Instagram—her thin, smooth-skinned ankles, her blue pumps. I feel the weight of the trouble we're in, but I also feel excited. I've always been the sort of person who functions best when she has a mess to clean up, a problem to solve, a mountain to move.

I have a habit of staring at people's feet on the train, imagining their life stories based on nothing but their shoes. The train stops at the next station and a flurry of people bustle in. I'm thinking of the millions of legs and ankles and shoes that trounce through the city everyday as the car grows more crowded.

Soon, my only choice is to look at the floor, otherwise I'd be staring at the crotches of the people standing around me.

There are men in tennis shoes and polished dress shoes as well as a guy with disgusting toenails wearing flip flops despite the temperature. I shudder. Then, about halfway up the now jampacked aisle, I see them. My eyes land on a pair of electric blue pumps. Are they hers? Is it April? My heart starts to race. I nudge Ted and he grasps my knee harder, probably thinking that the lurch of the train has pulled me into him.

"Those shoes," I whisper, just as the person belonging

to the feet stands.

I'm going to find out.

The car comes to a stop, and the feet in the blue pumps begin to move. I try to stand up, but I feel dizzy. I thrust my shoulders forward, but the mass of bodies keeps me locked in my seat.

"Are you okay?" Ted asks.

I feel a briefcase smash into my shoulder. Somebody steps on my toe.

She's getting away.

I'm not going to miss my chance. I press on Ted's leg for leverage and hurl myself forward, throwing my elbows.

"Where are you going? This isn't our stop," Ted says. "Elaine!" "Excuse me," I say, in my most booming voice. "Please let me out." "Elaine!" Ted tries to get up, but he's stuck in his seat by the crowd of people pushing through the aisles and the people shifting to let me out.

I'm being pushed into the sea of bodies down the aisle. I shove my way out of the door, past the rude people trying to board before everyone is out.

I scan the fast-moving feet of the commuters filling Union Station. My eyes fall on the stairs. I see the blue shoes ascending them and I run. I ignore the pain in my feet from these silly shoes and I leap up onto the first step and take them two at a time.

April. I have to get to April.

My lungs are burning from exertion and exhilaration and anger.

My body is full of adrenaline. A montage of terrible moments fills my brain.

Ted's hand on April's leg. Ted drinking wine with her. Then I think of myself waiting in my office like an idiot for the confirmation call from the Department of Justice and getting one from a reporter instead.

She's getting away.

I put all the force I can muster into my run and make it to the top of the stairs. The heavens shine down on me and April stops to retrieve something from her handbag. Briefly, I panic that she's spotted me and is calling the cops. Or Ted. Or Senator Montgomery.

I lunge toward her. At last, I catch up to the long-legged, sleek-suited brunette who is trying to ruin my life. I reach out to tap her back. I think about pulling her long, shiny mane. Instead I find myself swinging my purse at her. It connects with her skinny back, making a satisfying *whack.*

I blurt out, "Who in the hell do you think you are, April," just in time for her to turn around and reveal her face.

Which is not April's.

I feel sick to my stomach. *Oh, no. Holy shit.*

"Are you insane?" the woman shrieks, scared and puzzled.

"What's going on?" I hear a man ask through the phone she's carrying. "Jesus. Some crazy woman just hit me with her purse," she yelps into the phone. She's older than her body and shoes had signaled. Much closer to my age than April's.

"You're crazy! What's wrong with you?"

"I'm so sorry," I stammer. "Oh, my god. I … I thought you were someone else. I'm truly sorry.'

I am a complete idiot.

I back away and then turn and break into a run toward the opposite end of the station.

"You hit me," the woman yells after me. "You just came up to me and hit me. Who do you think you are?"

"Elaine!" I hear a man's voice yelling. For some reason, at first, I think it's the man on Not April's phone. Then I come to my senses and realize it's Ted.

I stop and wait for him, even though I'm so embarrassed. I want to sink into the floor. He reaches me and pulls me onto a bench. I feel conflicted, unsure of whether to be humiliated by my idiotic outburst or proud of myself. I've been wondering if I had the guts to confront April. Turns out I do! My neck and ears feel hot. I feel like I might cry. I can't believe I just did that. "What was *that*?" Ted asks.

"I thought she was April," I say quietly. I'm staring at the floor, too embarrassed to meet his eyes. "I just …"

"Elaine," he says. I look into his eyes and I can see that he's truly worried. "You can't go around hitting …." He pauses and takes my hand.

"I know," I say, sheepishly. This is humiliating.

"This is so unlike you."

"Of course, it's unlike me, Ted."

"I don't think I realized until now just how much this is affecting you."

How could he not realize? My phone rings, and I reach into my purse-turned-weapon to grab it.

"Hello," I say. I can hear breathing on the other end of the line, but no one speaks. "Hello? Who is this?" I feel the color drain from my face.

"What is it," Ted mouths.

"Hello," I yell. All I hear is breathing. I hang up.

"Are you okay," Ted asks.

"I'll be fine," I say, though I'm not sure how this will ever be true.

"I'm worried about you," Ted says. "I mean, you hit a woman with your purse."

"I know, I know," I say. "I actually *hit* that woman. And the sad part is that I can't stop thinking that she's lucky I didn't do worse!"

Together, Ted and I walk deliberately and silently into the crisp fall air. He dashes into CVS to get some bandages for the blisters that are already forming on my heels. I contemplate and wait in place until he returns and hands me the package.

"Thank you," I say. "I'll see you later at my office."

Ted looks dumbfounded as I hobble off to work. I should feel horrible and ashamed; instead, I feel invigorated. With every painful step, I find myself thinking that April McFarland is going down. Lorelei Montgomery is going down.

Jimmy Montgomery is going down.

"Long time, no see, ma'am," says Ellis, the security guard, as I limp into the building.

"I'm back!" I reply. And I *do* feel like I'm back. I feel morally stupid for having hit the wrong woman with my purse, of course. But I also feel brave for knowing that, if push comes to shove, I can and I will confront April.

I ride the elevator up to the eighth floor. Our suite is empty, and I feel a rush listening to my pinching black Louboutins clattering along the marble tile. In my office, I slide them off, feeling the relief from the tightness surge through me. I brew a pot of coffee, enjoying the rich aroma floating through the space. This has always been my favorite time of the day. I relish the quiet and the buzz of possibility of an early morning at the office. It's strange how exhilarated I feel.

Maybe a small part of me has always felt that the world was out to get me. It's a little ridiculous, I know, given all of my good fortune. But still. Maybe discovering April McFarland's plot means I can finally stop waiting for the worst!

Famous last words.

I pour myself a cup of what Ted likes to refer to as my rocket fuel. He likes watery coffee because his stomach is a mess from all the crap he eats. I love it strong and full-bodied. Jules jokes that I might as well just suck on the coffee filter and eat the grounds with a spoon. I'd probably like it, actually, and it sounds rather efficient. I sink into my ergonomically correct leather desk chair, an extravagance I'd protested but grown accustomed to. Story of my life!

I remove the photographs from the file folder inside my bag. I remember the cork board we used to keep in the old WRI office. I relished picking and choosing items from discovery files to pin to it. It indulged the courtroom-drama loving girl who'd decided to go to law school all those years ago. These days, Jules tries to get me to go digital with everything, and I ignore what she says; it's just not as satisfying.

I wheel the whiteboard I use for strategizing out of the closet. I don't care what Jules would think. Writing by hand is better!

The front side of the board is covered in a chart with each senator's name and their positions on my confirmation. Yeses in pink. Noes in black. Undecideds in purple. My eyes linger on Montgomery, in black. Our conversation at The Monocle comes back in a flood. *Why did he plant April McFarland? What is going on?*

"I don't know, but I'm going to get to the bottom of it," I say aloud to the empty office. I wheel the whiteboard around so I can use the blank side. I attach the three photos from my purse using the little magnets Jules always keeps on hand. I use a purple magnet for the photo of April and Lorelei, a red magnet for Mrs. Anna Strong's profile picture, and a blue magnet for the photo of April's feet. I draw an arrow between the electric blue pump on Anna's profile image and the electric blue pump on April's foot. My cheeks flush thinking of the feel of my purse connecting with that poor woman's back.

Suddenly, I have the urge to snap a picture of my feet

in the black pumps. But then I think about my old lady ankles—*cankles, ugh!* I wonder if April took the photo of the blue pumps on her commute. I wonder if Ted ever admired them. I wonder if he ever complimented them. If he ever fantasized about her wearing them in bed.

My heart sinks when I think of him flirting with her. When I replay what he said a few days ago. *I wanted to sleep with her. She's a beautiful young woman. She even reminds me a little of you.*

Before I can sink too deeply into the pit of self-pity, Jules appears in the doorway.

"What the hell is all of this," she asks. "Ew! Put your shoes on." She hates feet.

I walk around my desk and open the door where I keep my comfortable, sensible Tori Burch flats and slip into them.

"Give me a hug," Jules says. I'm kind of surprised because she's not really a hugger. She throws her arms around me, nearly spilling the coffee she's brought for me. Then her eyes turn to the whiteboard.

"It's insane," I say. "It's completely insane." I fill Jules in with most of the pertinent facts of what has been happening. She hesitates and within less than a minute, whips her phone out of her dress pocket and begins typing so fast it makes me dizzy.

"What are you doing," I ask.

"I'm sending these images to Jed," she says.

Jed is her boyfriend. "We need to keep this on the low down," I say. I don't know this Jed guy that well and now everyone is suspect. Everyone.

"It's *down low*," she says, not even bothering to look up from her phone. "And relax, I'm not texting him for nothing. He developed the facial recognition software for Facebook. He can tell us if that's the same foot."

"This is possible now," I ask, our code for my unending wonder at the speed of technological advancement. "There's an app for foot recognition?"

Jules grunts, her excuse for laughter. I hear her phone whoosh with the sound of outgoing texts. My stomach growls.

"I brought treats," Jules says. "Real ones. We can eat while we wait."

She rushes down the hall toward her desk to retrieve them. I settle into the oversized couch where clients usually sit. Jules sinks down next to me and unties the pastry box from *Je Ne Sais Quoi* on Connecticut Avenue.

I think of all the times that she and I have sat on this couch brainstorming.

Aside from the richness of the pastries, it feels like business as usual. But then again, the buttery croissant in my mouth could also be read as confirmation that the sky is falling. If it truly were any ol' day, we'd be eating vegan flaxseed muffins or sipping some kind of coconut water bullshit. She's letting me eat real food, so she must think we're screwed.

The flaky deliciousness melts in my mouth, and I sigh. Then, Jules's phone buzzes.

"It's the same foot," she says, mouth full of blueberry muffin. "It's definitely the same foot."

As I swallow the flaky croissant, I feel my throat tighten. I feel my stomach flutter. Muscle memory takes over as I recall choking on the green salad I was eating the day I got that fateful call. I feel the same twisted feeling.

Mrs. Anna Strong is April McFarland. April McFarland called me a woman scorned in her stupid little column. April McFarland.

Well, at least I can stop feeling bad about my desire to hit April with my purse! I do feel bad for her doppelgänger, though. I take a few deep breaths and calm down. I look at Jules. "Now what?"

Jules is already texting furiously. "Now," she says, "we call Shelby."

Shelby is the best private investigator in D.C. She's so good that nobody will admit to knowing her, yet she's the one everybody calls when they're in a pickle or when they need excellent opposition research.

Jules frowns at her phone as she texts. Her fingers are a blur. "Now," she says, just as Ted appears in the doorway earlier than expected, "we go to war."

I'm a little afraid of what will happen now that Jules sees Ted. If I were him, I'd probably duck.

"Hi," Ted says.

"You," Jules says, practically hissing. "Now, Jules …" I say halfheartedly. "What is he doing here?"

"We need him," I say.

"Correction," Jules says. "We need his *information.*"

To his credit, Ted seems to understand that this is not the time to defend himself.

"And I'm willing to share it," he says, perhaps a little too eagerly for someone like Jules. "What do you want to know?"

"I don't *want* to know anything, Ted," she says. "I *need* to know everything, but not right now."

In broad strokes, Jules erases the chart with the names tracking my pathway to confirmation. She ignores my yelp of dismay. I love that chart! I've been staring at that white board for months. I can't help but feel that she's erasing my dreams of judicial confirmation. I watch the eraser blur the names of the people who'd already promised to support my biggest career ambition. The Undecideds go next. Finally, the Noes. She wipes away Senator Montgomery.

"Adios, asshole," she says as his name disappears.

"Seriously," I say, trying to hide my sadness at the disappearance of my beloved chart. Then Jules turns to Ted and says it again. "Adios, asshole."

"You mean me?" Ted asks. I snort, trying not to laugh.

"Yes," Jules says. "Shelby's on her way over, and we need our privacy. You can wait in the other room."

She ushers Ted down the hall to the office where clients often hang out to wait for me. I can hear her showing him how to use the remote. She opens the mini fridge where we keep Diet Cokes and expensive bottled water.

When she returns, she surveys the strategy board.

With my dream wiped clean, Jules begins to make a list. She titles it GOALS. Before she can finish her first bullet point, the door to my office flies open, and I lift my eyes, expecting to find Shelby the Ace Private Investigator, but instead my mother-in-law enters the room, strides up to me on her sturdy elderly legs, and kisses me on both cheeks. She steps backward to look at me, nods her approval, and takes off her coat, handing it to Jules who eagerly anticipates the offering.

"Congresswoman?" Jules stammers, taking the garment, blushing. She sticks out her hand, only to get it caught inside the folds of Vivian's coat. "It's such a pleasure to meet you," she gushes, wrestling her hand free. "I've heard so much–"

"Coffee, dear," Vivian says to Jules, eyeing the pastry box, smiling placidly and reaching for a pain au chocolat. "Black, please! One sugar. Thanks. We have work to do."

Chapter Fourteen

The intercom on my desk buzzes. Ellis's voice fills the room.

"I have Shelby Wainright in the lobby," he says.

"Send her right up," I say, even though I'm nervous to see her. Nervous to hear what she'll think of the mess of my marriage. And she'll *definitely* tell me what she thinks. That's for sure. In the eighteen years I've known her, she's never once held back on her opinion. I hold my breath, and the elevator dings and Shelby appears.

Shelby Wainright looks like a Mormon grandmother. Her gray hair curls gently to frame her face. She's short and portly with sloping shoulders.

Everything about her is soft and gentle, except for her wit, except for the switchblade she always carries on her person, and except for her commitment to justice.

Shelby has been my eyes and ears for a decade now. She has spied on clients who seemed sympathetic on paper but made my hackles go up in person. She's tailed defendant after defendant, turning up mistresses and hidden financial lives. One time, she discovered a prominent tech CEO's intimate relationship with his first cousin. Before she went on a second date with her facial recognition guru boyfriend, Jules sent Shelby after him. Obviously, he came up clean.

Shelby holds me at arm's length, the way grandmas so often do. As if to say *let me get a good look at you — my how you've grown.*

"You look like a pile of shit," Shelby says. There's her trademark honesty. Well, I guess it's not actually honesty that's her trademark, since she's willing to lie through her teeth to get what she needs. "Do I need a bagman for your eyes? Jules, get this woman some cucumbers for god's sake!"

Jules laughs and says, "I know, right?" I can't believe I pay these people to talk to me this way, but I chuckle, too.

My mother-in-law clatters her coffee cup against the saucer, and we all turn to look at her.

"Vivian," says Shelby. Her tone is decidedly not warm.

"Shelby," says Vivian, equally coolly.

"You two know each other?" I say.

"Democratic primary, 1998," Shelby says.

"She provided opposition research," Vivian informs us.

"Excellent," chirps Jules. "So you've worked together before!" I'm astonished at the sudden personality shift my assistant seems to have undergone in the last ten minutes. She's positively bubbly. Eager to please, almost obsequious. *Oh my god*, I realize. *She's intimidated. By Vivian.*

"We didn't exactly work together," Shelby says.

Viv lets out a snort. I glance from one to the other. Their expressions are flat, unreadable.

"Shelby, you did oppo research on Vivian!" I can't help myself: I laugh out loud. "What a small city this is."

"She found nothing," Vivian says. "Just for the record."

"She's right," Shelby replies, giving me a broad, obvious wink. "I found absolutely nothing whatsoever."

Vivian clatters her cup and saucer again.

"Elaine, you really look like shit," Shelby reiterates.

"Her intern needs to quit buying her French pastries," Vivian observes. She turns toward Jules. "Sweetie, there's a vegan bakery around the corner. They make a delicious flaxseed muffin."

"I'm not an intern, ma'am, I'm Elaine's executive assist–"

Vivian raises her hand in a Queen Mother gesture, apparently oblivious to her error, and Jules goes instantly silent. I wonder if I could start getting her to treat me with this kind of respect, but realize it is far too late.

"I know I look like shit," I reply. She's right. Actually, she's being kind. I look worse than shit. "It's been …" I stammer.

"Hell?" "Exactly," I say.

"Ted's not here, is he?"

"He's in the other room. Waiting for us until we need him," Jules says. "What?" Vivian says to me. "Why have you put your husband in another room? Are we not all on the same team here? Is he being punished? Like a little boy?"

"We needed some privacy…" Jules murmurs.

Vivian fixes Jules with a blank stare and then turns to me. "Do you always let your intern call the shots?"

"She's my assistant," I say. Which Vivian knows very well, of course. Then, feeling bad for Jules, I add: "She's more like my chief of staff, to be honest."

Jules straightens in her chair and suppresses a tiny smile.

"You have a staff?" Vivian replies, knowing full well that I don't, and then she finally breaks her ice queen routine and shoots a playful look at Jules, who gapes back at her in astonishment. Vivian smiles warmly toward her and gives a thumbs up. Jules is beaming and does the same. I am stupefied by both of them.

"We'll invite Ted into the discussion as soon as we need his information," says Shelby.

"I'm going to suggest we need him right this minute," Vivian replies. "You're like a bunch of mommies trying to send a grown man to his room. We need to discuss this like adults."

"What I need," Shelby says, "is to wring his neck and kick his sorry …" She starts for the hallway, presumably to go find Ted.

I put my hand on her shoulder, thinking of her damn switchblade. I'm not taking any chances. "We need Ted alive, Shel," I say, only half joking.

"Hey, Mom," Ted says as he enters the room, all confidence and swagger. This is a boy who knows his mother will always love him no matter what. Under any circumstances. Regardless of what he's done, she'll defend him to the death. Ted could drown a bag of kittens in her toilet. He could embezzle from the Girl Scouts. He could take a long naked piss on her front lawn. Which he did, once, at the age of seventeen, after a drunken night out with the kids from the Young Democrats. When his adventure landed her in the gossip pages – a spiteful neighbor documented the moment – she laughed at the reporter's question about public exposure laws and suggested the media was just slightly too invested in the status of her son's penis.

"Tell me, son," Vivian says. "Did you behave inappropriately with that young woman?"

"No, ma'am," Ted responds.

Vivian beams at him. "Well then," she says, "that settles that." Good god, her blind spot for her son's weaknesses could hide an elephant. Jules is twitching like a meth addict, caught between her anger at Ted and her fear of his mother.

She wants to say something so badly I can practically hear her thoughts.

Shelby surveys the bullet points on Jules' strategy board and groans. "How many times do I have to tell you to leave the investigating to the investigator?

None of that's going to work. In fact, that's probably exactly what they want." She spins the board around and looks at the photos.

"Where's your confirmation chart?" Vivian asks.

Still stung by the loss, I point my finger at Jules. "Erased."

"Well that's a damn shame," Vivian says.

"It's okay," Jules says. "I took a picture." She swipes and pokes at her phone, finds what she's looking for, and then hands it to Viv. "Here, just tap twice on the part of the picture you want magnified–"

"I know how a smartphone works," Vivian says, handing it back to Jules. "And I also know how a smartphone doesn't work. For one thing, it doesn't work like a whiteboard. Not even close. A whiteboard is big, for example, and this fucking thing is tiny."

"I'm sorry, I–" Jules says.

"When I said it's a damn shame, I meant it's a damn shame that we're going to have to write it out all over again. We're going to need to stare at it for a while."

"Viv," I say. "Listen, that's not necessary, really...I can fill you in, I know the chart by heart anyway."

"No," Jules says, grabbing a dry erase marker. "She's right. This whole thing with April McFarland might have everything to do with your nomination. We need to look at it all over again, through a new lens." Jules approaches the board, wheels it back around so the white side faces us and begins drawing columns.

"Atta girl," Vivian tells her.

Shelby has followed the board in a half circle, still studying the photos pinned to the corkboard side. Her support hose and sensible shoes – does she shop at nursing uniform shops for those things? – are all that we can see of her.

"Well, then what are we going to do, Shelby?" I ask,

feeling comforted by the fact that Shelby *always* has a plan. I don't know why I didn't call her as soon as I hung up the phone with that reporter.

"First things first." Shelby swings the board around, ignoring Jules' yelp of protest as she's relegated to the blind side. Shelby puts on the reading glasses that hang on the little jeweled string around her neck. She takes down the photos of Mrs. Anna Strong and April McFarland.

She clears her throat. Then she sighs dramatically. "Ted," she says.

"Yes, Shelby," he replies.

"Given that your former colleague April McFarland has turned out to be the city's most infamous gossip blogger, how would you rate yourself as a judge of character?"

"Shelby," says Vivian. "A bit of civility–"

"Christ, Mom, I can speak for myself," Ted finally says.

Vivian slides back in her seat and throws up her hands in an okay-fine-I'm-backing-off gesture.

"Relevance of the question," Ted asks Shelby.

"Just determining how much weight we should give to your response to my next question," Shelby replies, "considering that all evidence tells us that the courtroom where your internal judge of character presides is located at the tip of your dick." She glares at his crotch, in full view given he'd manspread himself all over the place.

From behind the barrier of the whiteboard, Jules guffaws heartily and stamps her foot. I can hear her marker flying over the whiteboard, making what I know are perfectly legible letters. Spelling out my yesses and noes and maybes.

Is there nothing this woman isn't good at? Patience, I suppose. She's impatient as hell.

Ted crosses his legs defensively. He turns to me. "You did actually tell them that I'm innocent, didn't you?"

I'm not ready to give Ted a pass, nor will I defend him in front of these women. My colleagues. His mother. No, let him face the consequences. He let himself be seduced by a pretty girl with ulterior motives. It was as though he had simply switched off his celebrated strategic man brain and turned into a horny fourteen year old. I first started seeing Hillary Clinton as a role model back in the 90's, when she told the cameras she wasn't going to be anything like Tammy Wynette, just standin' by her man.

"I told them you didn't sleep with her, if that's what you mean," I say to my husband.

"Exactly!" he says, cutting the air with his hand. I cringe, seeing he's missed the point entirely, and they're about to take off his head. Yet he continues. "So how about you ladies lay off already, cut me some slack?"

"No can do, counselor," says Shelby. "You're in the hotseat, so you'd just better put an icepack on those cojones and get used to the discomfort. You might think you're getting 'caught up' in some kind of bad political moment, but you'll get no tears from us on that score. You and yours have been benefitting from the rape culture all your damn lives, and therefore your sole proper response to these allegations is to pretend to be a recently awakened humble male feminist. For the sake of your wife's career, we will coach you through this persona, unrelentingly, until you embody the principles rather than just repeat them like some puppet dude who has no idea what he's talking about."

"Hashtag me too!" chirps Jules, over the squeak of her dry-erase markers. "Clear your schedule. For coming weeks," continues Shelby, "you will be undergoing Gender Studies Boot Camp at the National Women's Public Relations Academy."

"Is that a thing?" Ted says.

"I don't think so, honey," I tell him.

Vivian reaches over to Ted and places her hand over

his. "I think what they're saying, dear, is if you can't take the heat, it's best you get out of our kitchen."

"Jesus Christ you women are killing me," Ted says. "So what's your actual question, Shelby?"

"My question?" Shelby rocks dramatically back on her heels, a move made possible only by those comfortable ugly shoes. Finally she blurts it out. "What does April McFarland want, Ted?"

From behind the whiteboard comes the voice of Jules, blurting "...besides your hot bod?"

"All right," Ted says. "I get it. I'm a rape culture opportunist. But this isn't getting us anywhere. Listen, April duped me. She flirted, she suggested, she made it known she was interested, and I believed her, and the whole thing turned me inside out. Yes, my judgment was obviously impaired. Yes, I was flattered. No, I didn't see that she was working for the enemy. But honestly I did see something... that was not quite right."

"In what way?" I say, meeting his gaze. "Honestly."

"In the very few moments when we would acknowledge openly what was going on between us – or, at least, what I thought was going on – she would touch me, just rest her hand on my arm or my leg, and a moment like that ought to feel electric, you know? But her touch didn't feel..."

Ted trailed off, and for once none of the four women facing him had anything to say. We knew what he meant. He meant April was pretending, and on some level he knew it even when it was happening, and my heart melted for him just a little bit, because he must be feeling humiliated and foolish, like the skinny freshman who's been cruelly led on by the captain of the cheerleading squad.

"Anyway, I suppose they would call a mistrial if the Montgomery case was being tried now," I ask him, "given your office has been infiltrated by the opposition?"

"Hey, couldn't April then be held in contempt of court," says Jules, "for feeding information to the defendant?"

"Atta girl," says Vivian. "She's right. April's legal career is on the line." "Ladies and non-ladies," Shelby announces, nodding at Ted, "we have our plan!"

"Spit it out already, lady," says Jules.

"The answer is as elegant as it is simple," Shelby tell us. "It's only a matter of outing our dear Mrs. Anna Strong."

Chapter Fifteen

By the time Jules finally turns the whiteboard around to reveal my confirmation chart, restored to its former glory, Ted has already left, late for a press interview, and Shelby is long gone, presumably off to rescue or to wreck another inside-the-beltway career.

"Okay, you two," I say to Vivian and Jules, who are standing side by side with their backs to me, staring at my chart. "I'm going into my office to take a nap. I'm visiting a client out at Bethesda this afternoon." I don't mention my other reason for a trip to the prison, which is to buy off the inmate that Frank Francis wants silenced.

"Okay, sweetie, good idea," says Vivian, without turning around.

"How will you..." I say.

"I'll make sure she gets home okay," interrupts Jules, waving me off. "Go take a nap, you seriously need one. Draw the shades. I'll hold your calls."

My hand is on the doorknob when Jules calls out for me to wait a minute. "What about Frank Francis," she asks. She's hopped up on political adrenaline, excited to be standing next to the legendary Vivian the Great. "On my phone, it looked like you'd erased the NO? But he's not a YES, either? Is he a maybe? What's up?"

"He's a YES," I tell them.

"Really?" says Vivian. She knows about my college thing with him. Ted told her, of course.

"Jules, don't wear Vivian out," I tell her. It's easy to forget the woman is 85 years old.

"How did you pull it off?" Jules asks.

"What, Francis? You don't want to know," I say. "Trust me, just don't ask."

To my relief, Jules shrugs her shoulders and turns back to the chart. Vivian eyes me as if to say, *we'll discuss this later, young lady.*

I head for the couch in my office, leaving my assistant and my mentor standing before my confirmation chart, their heads tilted together, pointing at Senators' names and talking together in low voices.

I sleep like a drunken log, and am awakened by a call from the car service, confirming my pickup in ten minutes for the ride to Bethesda Prison.

I hate visiting the prison. It's a full hour drive, first

of all, and the last thing I need right now is that much quiet. Even though I've already napped, I pass out almost instantly and, somewhat embarrassingly, wake myself up snoring.

Bethesda Minimum Security Prison isn't the worst place on earth to land. Nor is it the best. I've been in prisons unfit for anyone, guilty or not. We pass the sign labeled Hopewell Road. I wonder what came first — the street or the prison. The building itself is squat, nondescript, and dreary beige with drain pipes every ten feet. To either side of the entrance, there's a small patch of technicolor green grass. The outside is bad enough, but it's what's inside that's so awful.

The guards.

They prefer to be called correction officers. Bullshit. There is little to no effort to reform or rehabilitate. Purely punitive punishment.

They buzz me in, and I'm escorted to a small, dingy conference room. I sit on one of the two folding chairs at a card table.

Elena looks haggard. Exhausted. Sad. The way I've only ever seen her after we lost an appeal.

On the way home last night, I stopped and bought Elena two Mr. Goodbar candy bars, and threw them in my briefcase. They're her favorite, and she usually tears the first one open like a kid on Christmas morning and gobbles it up. The second one, she savors, breaking it into squares and letting them melt on her tongue as I update her on strategy.

Today, when I put them on the table, she doesn't touch them.

"Bad night," I ask. She looks as tired as she looked in the earliest days of her time behind bars. Back when the sound of the other inmates crying or snoring or hooking up kept her awake. Within two weeks, she was sleeping again. It's amazing what the body can adapt to.

"There was a ruckus," she says.

"A ruckus," I say, side-eyeing the guard. I've always told clients that prison is all about chickenshit rules enforced by chickenshit people. The first time I visited a client, I cried the whole way home. A guard took the care package I'd painstakingly assembled. He ripped open the bag of Doritos and ate them. He dumped the super absorbency tampons in the trash. Now, I know better. I bring whatever the client can eat in the course of a meeting and I keep their commissary account stocked. They only take money orders. Every month, I add $50 to Elena's account. I'm not being cheap. If there's too much in there, word will get out, and she'll be bullied and threatened into buying packs of cigarettes and pads.

Prison is a place that runs on two things: hope that time will pass fast and desperation to meet basic needs.

"Things got crazy ..." her eyes wander to the guard. He is standing outside the door, but he's looking into the window through the honeycomb wired glass.

"Count?" I whisper, thinking of the report I'd filed two years ago after the guards had ordered a headcount in the middle of the night. They'd trashed Elena's cell block at three a.m. and flashed lights in the women's faces for three hours because someone sneezed during the count when they were supposed to freeze and be completely silent.

Elena shakes her head. The guard is looking at us with contempt. The ones they send to guard the meetings with the lawyers are always the worst. They love the power trip. They love to eavesdrop and use whatever they glean against the women.

He's probably friends with one of the animals who once took away Elena's bed linens as punishment for rolling her eyes at him. Elena reaches for the candy and delicately peels the yellow paper away from the foil. Happy to see her eating, I smile.

The guard seems to think I'm smiling at him. He looks at me, scans my upper body, and, almost imperceptibly, winks. Fucker.

"It's Sammy," Elena whispers. Her eyes fill with tears. I haven't seen her cry much, so I'm taken aback. I offer her a tissue from my purse and touch her arm.

"Watch the physical contact, counselor," Captain Fucker says.

My stomach drops at the mention of Sammy's name. I am not used to half-assing. But I've been half-assing everything with Elena. Whatever she's about to tell me is something I should have seen coming, I'm sure. Oh, the irony of trying to save my career while phoning it in with my clients!

"It's horrible," she says. She tells me that they let Sally out of solitary. That she was ordered to stay away from Sammy, but they took one look at one another across the cafeteria and to hell with the rules. Sally could tell something was wrong with Sammy. And she was right, Elena said. Nobody knew exactly what happened, but one of the guards had done something terrible to Sammy while Sally was in solitary.

"The way they looked at each other," Elena says. She trails off. She rolls up the sleeve of the white prison-issue undershirt she has on under her scrubs. I see that her arm is dotted with small bruises, like the spots on a fawn's fur.

I reach for her again, mentally willing that jerk

outside to come in and just try me. "What the hell, Elena," I say. "What happened?"

"I'm getting to it," she says. "So they found each other when we went out in the yard. They were trying to use friends to relay messages to each other. But then they just couldn't stand it anymore."

Sally and Sammy went off to a corner that was somewhat of a blind spot to the guards. Sally leaned into Sammy and whispered something in her ear.

"We were all huddled around them," Elena says. "Kinda clustering up in that way that the guards don't like. The way that brings down a real ass-kicking.

We shoulda known. But Sally just gets so messed up when she has to go to solitary. She came out just looking like a crazed animal and ...." Elena is saying. I have a feeling that these details are supposed to resonate with me, are something I'm already supposed to know but only vaguely recall. Again, I vow to be more present for Elena.

"How long was she in there for," I ask. There are rules that have to be followed. I could make a report or something. Nothing ever comes of them on their own, but it's still good to build a case. Maybe someday I'll take these assholes on. If my reputation doesn't go down the toilet.

"This is gonna sound super weird. But I saw Sally whispering in Sammy's ear. I was watching their faces together. Thinking, you know, you're in this place, and it's so crowded, but you could go crazy with loneliness. You could lose your damn mind wanting someone to touch you." Elena pauses and makes a face. "You just miss a touch. You know what I miss? I miss getting a haircut every six weeks. The smell of the shampoo. I never even went to nice places, just Super Cuts. I bet you go to a nice place," she says.

Instinctively, I smooth my hair. "I spend way too much money on things like that," I say sheepishly.

Elena laughs. "So, anyway, Sammy and Sally had their heads together.

Sammy's mouth was so close to Sally's ear, and I just had this vision of Sammy sticking her tongue out and licking it. I guess I must have closed my eyes and then when I opened them ..."

The guard is supposed to stay right outside the door. This is a minimum security joint, after all. But I hear the door buzz open.

"Ten-minute warning," he says.

"We're supposed to have an hour," I tell him.

"Well, is that so," he says. My neck prickles, the way it does when Bernice, my stylist, sweeps the back of my neck with a brush to dust off the hair. He's going to give me shit, isn't he?

"Yes," I say, "I'm entitled to an hour with my client. You need to check the paperwork," I say, looking at his nametag, "Ed-Is-It?" I make a show of shuffling folders in my briefcase. But apart from the nondisclosure agreement and the check for $5,000 I've brought to present to the inmate attacked by Francis's nephew – one Samantha Gonzalez – I really don't have any paperwork.

"Well, today, the paperwork says thirty minutes. Somebody else needs this room." Dickwad. He buzzes himself out, and the door closes. The lock clicks. I suddenly feel claustrophobic and sweaty. I wish I could unbutton my blouse.

"So I open my eyes, and all hell has broken loose," Elena says. The guards are hitting people, and everyone is yelling. I didn't see it, but one of the guards busted through the crowd of us. He shoved Sally and Sammy's heads together, so hard Sammy bit her tongue and blood was squirting out of it. I know what you gotta do at that moment. You gotta freeze. You gotta sink down to the ground and protect your head. So I did."

"They pulled you up? Those bruises? They're fingerprints?"

"Yes," she says. "It could have been a lot worse."

"Are Sammy and Sally in solitary now?"

The door buzzes. The guard comes in. "Times up."

"There's no way it's been ten minutes, Ed," I say.

"Well, my watch says otherwise," he hisses.

Before I can protest – my client and I haven't even discussed her case! – he's cuffing Elena and ushering her out of the room. The door buzzes and shuts behind him. For a moment, I'm stuck. I gather my things. I imagine Elena going back to her cell block. I imagine she and her friend plotting. I imagine Sally and Sammy together in the yard. Aching for each other's touch. Desperate to be near each other.

I have a flashback of April McFarland's face against Lorelai's ear. Of her long wavy locks touching Lorelei's bare shoulders.

I take the photo of April and Lorelai out of my briefcase again and study it, desperate for clues. I search April and Lorelei's faces. April's hands protectively around Lorelai's middle.

The guard returns and buzzes me out. The intake personnel return my cell phone. My meeting for the Francis payoff isn't for another 45 minutes. I stand outside in the parking lot, pacing and thinking.

I'm not sure what the hell it means, but I'm suddenly

wondering if April McFarland is in love with Lorelei Montgomery.

Am I insane? Could it really be as simple as that? As simple as romance?

There was something about April's hand on Lorelei's belly. Something about the way she looked at Lorelei. Something.

Chapter Sixteen

I feel a hand on the small of my back. At first, I think it's that smarmy guard, and I'm ready to go into attack mode. I jump.

I turn around to find a handsome young man I know I've seen before. I wrack my brain and realize it's Aiden Cross. He worked for Ted as an intern. I always wanted to smack the smug look off his face. But I also wanted to see him shirtless. If I were a different kind of woman…

"Elaine!" he says, though I've never given him permission not to call me Ms., much less to touch my back.

"Hi, Aiden," I say. "What brings you here?"

"Oh, just visiting my girlfriend."

"Very funny."

"Clients, you know?"

I do know. I've had 'clients, you know,' since this little prick was in diapers.

"Same here." I scan the parking lot looking for my driver, hoping to hide in the backseat of my car away from this annoying youth. Maybe my driver has hung around and is not off somewhere finding a decent cup of coffee. No such luck. The driver is nowhere in sight.

"My client is in trouble with the guards," Aiden blurts out.

Who does that? Everyone knows that 'what brings you here', is small talk like 'how are you', not 'excuse me, what are all of the many intimate details of your case?'

"That's too bad," I say hoping to shut it down.

"Yeah," Aiden says. "They beat up her, uh, girlfriend, I suppose you'd call her, stuck her in solitary, and my client mouthed off to a guard..."

My ears perk up. I should stop him. An ethical person would stop him, right? He's got to be talking about Sally. Or Sammy. Instead, I force on my please, please, tell me more face. The one I wear whenever someone is about to walk into a trap and voluntarily tell me what I need to know. It's just that it's usually a witness. Not someone shitting on attorney-client privilege.

"Oh," I say, arching my brows.

"Yeah, she was flirting with one of these guards to get extra stuff. Like they do, you know?"

His tone makes me want to slap him. What 'extra stuff' does he even mean? Tampons? Deodorant? A cold

Dr. Pepper from the staff vending machine? How dare she do what she has to do to make her time for a non-violent drug trafficking offense, even a tiny bit better? And which was it? Was she mouthing off, or flirting?

"These ladies can be very manipulative and ...." he says. I'm willing my eyes not to roll, so he'll keep talking, and I can figure out what Elena was trying to tell me. Not that he has enough sense to know he's displeasing a 'lady'. I concentrate on watching his perfectly symmetrical face. His strong jawline. His perfect-but-not-too perfect hair. I feel terrible for Sally or Sammy or whichever one he's representing. A guy like this can be as mediocre as he wants. And get away with it.

"Oh, I don't know about that." I say, and I'm immediately grossed out by how playful I sound. Is this what April did to Ted?

"Anyway, now she's crying rape."

Now I don't have a lot of phrases that trigger me. But this one does. It makes me turn into the upper middle class white lady version of The Hulk. I feel like I'm going to burst out of my tailored blazer. Plus, I'm realizing, as belatedly as humanly possible, that Elena's friend Sammy is in fact Samantha Gonzalez, the same woman I'm here to see. The same woman Frank Francis is prepared to pay off with a scandalous five thousand bucks to keep silent about being sexually assaulted by a prison guard.

"Well," I say, trying not to lose my shit, "if she's had sex with anyone who works for the prison, she's been raped. Period. The law is very clear about that. Imprisoned people can't give consent."

"If anything even happened. What if she's just mad about him breaking up her little lesbian lovefest or whatever? Should a guy really lose his job over that? Should his life really be ruined," he says.

"People lose their job for taking home printer paper and computer chargers. Technically, he should lose his job for giving her a Coke from the vending machine…"

"So I don't want to be awkward, but I heard about Ted," Aiden says. "You know, about what she's saying about him."

"Oh," I say, "yes, that." Understatement of the year!

"You know I never liked her," Aiden says. "Very stuck-up."

"Wait a minute … you know her?"

"Yeah," he says. "We were at American together for undergrad. She lived on my floor second year. Then in our junior year, a bunch of us rented a big duplex. Me, a couple buddies, her, her friend, Lo, and some other chick… I forget her name, but she was kinda goth like, just black lipstick and everything but she moved out because my roommate Dan slept with her and then was a total dick to her."

I nod at Aiden's incessant babbling. My mind stops on Lo. Lo. What is that name? Why am I so stuck on that name?

"Lo was like super super Christian," he says. "All that Bible-thumping and she never really brought anyone home to, you know..."

I put my hand on Aiden's arm. "Wait a minute, Lo isn't by any chance ...."

"Married to a senator now?" he asks. "Yeah, the really old one," he says. "I always forget whether it's Hatch or Montgomery."

"It's Montgomery," I say. I could kiss this kid. This dumb babbling good-looking kid.

"Shit," Aiden says. The alarm on the Apple Watch he's wearing beeps. I shiver. It's turned cold. The sky is gray and the clouds look heavy with rain.

"I'm five minutes late." He goes in for a hug. His lips land on my cheek, leaving a wet spot. The hairs on the back of my neck stand up. "It was so good to see you, Elyse," he says, talking to my chest instead of my face. "Tell the old ball and chain I say hello."

"It's Elaine, asshole," I mutter when he's out of

earshot.

I'm not proud to do it, but I watch Aiden as he walks toward the door. Why does such a sexist pig get to have a butt like that? He's wearing one of those cross-body manbags. There's a Bernie Sanders button on it. Because of course there is.

Through the window, I can see him talking to the intake guard. I bet the guards don't give him shit. I bet their watches don't say a different time for him.

I want to run after him and whack him with my purse as I did the lady I thought was April. My face flushes at the memory of the woman's stunned face. I'm so embarrassed. I'm such a hypocrite. Thinking of hitting someone for saying a woman is 'calling rape' when, if I'm being honest, that's what I always suspected April of doing. The shadier she gets and the more evident it seems that she's knee-deep in some kind of bizarre plot, the easier it is to minimize the way I questioned her story from the start.

I pull out my phone and call the office of Frank Francis. When I tell his secretary who I am and that I'm standing outside the prison, she tells me Frank will call me right back.

"Frank," I say when he calls, presumably from his personal cell phone. "Bad news. This thing with your nephew is going to cost you more than five grand. A lot more."

"Jesus Christ," he whispers.

"I've just met with the complainant," I lie. "She's got a solid case.

Witnesses. Plus –" and this part is actually the truth, dug up by Shelby – "your deadbeat relative already has two strikes against him. He's been disciplined twice in the past year for inappropriate conduct with prisoners. Third assault, he's looking at jail time."

I think of myself sitting on the federal bench. Judge Elaine Bower Camden.

Judges aren't supposed to lie. Judges are supposed to be the most honest and principled humans in society. Fortunately, I'm not a judge yet. "Also she's got a damn good lawyer. Hot shit wonder kid named Aiden something. Used to work for Ted, in fact. You know him?"

"What's her price?" Frank says.

I don't hesitate. "Fifty thousand, plus early release. And your nephew quits prison work."

He grunts. "Fine." The loss of that kind of cash will cause him no pain, other than greater irritation with his sister's no-good kid. Me, I can't wait to go inside that prison and tell a woman who's been raped that she's getting out of lockup, and moreover hand her a down payment on a house of her own. A place that's all hers, so that someday, finally, she and Sally can be together.

"One more thing, Frank," I say. "You're still on the judiciary committee?"

He exhales into the phone, exasperated. "You know that I am, Elaine. What do you want?"

"Make a call," I say. "Get a case dismissed. Call off the D.A. It's a drug charge, nonviolent. Victimless."

"And tell me, why should I do this for you? Just for old times' sake? I'd have to pull a lot of strings."

"Yes. For old times."

I listen to the silence on the phone for a few seconds, then I say, "and also there's a certain gossip blogger, the one with famous legs, you know who I mean?"

"Of course I know who you mean. I don't live under a rock."

"I've recently come to learn her identity. We were talking yesterday, and your name came up." As a liar, I am on such a roll. I hereby vow, I tell myself, to live a life of excruciating honesty. Starting tomorrow. "I thought I should warn you, Frank, she's considering a column. Something about gay bathhouses."

Listen, I know some people would be mortified at what I'm doing here. I'm one of those people! Who we sleep with is nobody's business but our own, and nobody deserves to have their most intimate sexy time details hung out for the world to see.

Unless you're backing legislation to deny people their rights based on who they sleep with. Which, sadly for him, Frank Francis is currently doing. He was cosponsor of SB 4033, a bill that would allow employers to fire people based on "abnormal" gender expression, even if they, like Frank Francis, only practiced such deviant behaviors behind closed doors.

Frank sighs. I get the feeling he's dealt with these kinds of moments before. "And let me guess. You can convince this blogger to abandon that particular subject?"

"I can give it a try," I say.

"What's the name," Frank asks, and for a moment I think he wants me to give him the identity of Anna Strong. But then I realize he wants the name of my client, the name of the case to be dismissed.

"Morales," I tell him. "Elena Morales."

Chapter Seventeen

When I get home I'm exhausted. It's been an incredibly long day and yet I still have to meet Shelby at the Monocle. I don the disguise she messengered to my house and head to the restaurant. I take a barstool in a dark corner next to Shelby, also in disguise. I'm wearing a wig, a scarf, and a thick pair of horn-rimmed glasses. I feel fucking ridiculous and sick with nerves. How has my life come to this? How am I wearing a costume in public, for god's sake?

Shelby's wearing a dark brown wig with bangs, which is absurd because April doesn't even know her. For some reason, she's also added a chunky set of fake pearls. She looks as silly as I feel.

From our vantage point, we can see Jules, waiting at a dining table. She looks carefree and composed, as usual.

The brick red Birkin bag I gave her last Christmas sits on one of the spare chairs. Inside it there's a file folder containing the photos of April's feet and Mrs. Anna

Strong's profile pic and a printout of image analysis data from her Facebook genius beau, everything she needs to corner April McFarland. Also in the bag is a microphone, courtesy of Shelby. The waiter arrives and Jules orders two martinis extra dry, a shrimp cocktail, and a bread basket. When he brings the drinks, she takes one and arranges the other at the place across from her. She looks professional and confident. Like she could be waiting for a date.

I'm trying not to look at her obsessively. I don't want to draw attention to her. My stomach flutters nervously. I look so incredibly ridiculous in this getup.

Why the hell did I want to come? I should have stayed home like Shelby suggested. What if I lose control when April arrives? What if I rip off my disguise and tackle her? How satisfying it would feel to get a fistful of her hair!

As soon as I imagine that scene, I chastise myself. *You still don't know the full story, Elaine,* I think. It's true. I don't. It's entirely possible that April is telling the truth. Just because she's probably working for Jimmy Montgomery doesn't automatically mean she lied. I hate this! I hate still doubting my husband! I hate feeling like a woman scorned. I hate heaping contempt on another woman.

I hate it!

The waiter returns with Jules' food. She selects a juicy pink shrimp and dips it in cocktail sauce. I watch it disappear into her mouth. She drops the tail on a small white saucer. I feel like that shrimp. Chewed up. Nothing left of me but a discarded shell.

What if April doesn't come at all? What if she's onto us? What if she sees right through Jules' cover? What if she doesn't believe that Jules is a reporter, writing a story on the culture of rampant sexual harassment in D.C.?

The host is leading someone up the steps.

It's April. Her luxurious waves bounce against her shoulders as she climbs.

I can tell even from several yards away that her skin is smooth, clear, and glowing. I feel like someone punched me in the stomach. Who does she think she is with that body? With those legs?

She's beautiful.

Instinctively, I look at her feet. She's wearing pumps. But they're red, not blue. I feel like time has stopped. The blood in my veins stops cold. I pick up the drink Shelby has ordered for me and gulp it down. The chill of the drink clatters against my teeth. I swallow and the booze stifles my immediate thought process. I begin to choke up as I did when I received that first phone call.

What do you have to say about April McFarland's allegations?

I need to be in control. I sit statue still and tap at the tiny speaker in my left ear, my link to the bug in the Birkin. Everything seems to happen in slow motion.

Jules rises to greet April and shake her hand.

"Andrea Maclean," she says, using the fake name we agreed upon. "Nice to meet you," April says, and offers a little smile.

Jules sits. The host pulls April's chair out. She sits, lifts her round-but-not-too-round bottom ever so slightly, and he delicately pushes her in.

"Thank you for coming," Jules says.

"No problem," April replies. It drives me insane when young people say that. I always tell Kendall not to do it. The only appropriate response to '*thank you*' is '*you're welcome*'.

"For me," April asks, gesturing to the drink. Jules nods and April takes a generous sip. I kind of wish it were laced.

"So," Jules says, her hands moving deftly to the Birkin bag. Oh, god, I think, our lie is so awful. What twenty-five-year-old journalist can afford a Birkin bag?

"Great bag," April says. "May I see it?"

"Thank you. It was a gift." Jules says. She retrieves

the file folder from the purse and hands the purse to April.

I tense up in my seat, exchanging a look with Shelby. She pats my knee confidently. What if April looks in Jules' bag? What if she sees the badge for my building or Jules' driver's license or …. the goddamn microphone?

"Great color," April says. "So versatile." She hands the bag back to Jules.

She seems so earnest. I wonder if it's part of her act. I wonder, irrationally, if she knows that this is all a set-up and is just trying to torture me.

"Yes," Jules says, curtly. I can tell by her face that she's getting impatient. I can also tell that even though she said the exact same thing about the bag when I gave it to her, she thinks April's a daft cow.

"Anyway, let's get down to business," Jules continues. "Shall we, Mrs. Strong?"

I nearly spit out my drink. April's face goes white. Jules slides the file folder across the table.

"Excuse me …" April says. "I …"

"Drop the act," Jules says. "I know exactly who you are, and I have the analytics to prove it. You're busted."

"I don't know what you're talking about," April says.

"Oh, I think you do." She opens the folder and fans the documents out for April to see.

"Where did you get this?" April stammers.

"I'd think you'd be more interested in *what* I'm going to do with it," Jules says.

"What're ... you can't ... prove anything ..." April mumbles, just as her eyes fall on the evidence that Jules can, in fact, prove everything.

"Oh, I think you can see that I can, darling," Jules says. Beside me, Shelby lets out a soft snort.

"What do you want," April asks, her voice rising an octave.

"What do I want," Jules says, slowly and calmly. She leans back into her chair. God, she was born for this kind of thing! Shelby jabs me in the ribs as if to say *get a load of this!* She drains the rest of her martini.

April begins to speak, "I ..."

Jules cuts her off. She signals to the waiter. "Well, first, I want another drink."

"And then," April asks weakly.

"And then I want your cooperation."

"With what?"

"Here's how it's going to go down," Jules says. "You're going to tell me everything you know about Senator Montgomery, and you're going to tell me now."

"Or ..." April says. Her face is frozen in a deliberately blank look. I can't tell if she's shocked or awed or getting ready to laugh out loud.

"Or I will call every single person in Washington D.C. who's wound up on your stupid little gossip blog and give them your home address," Jules says.

April starts to stand up, seems to think better of it, and sits down.

"And I won't stop there," Jules promises, just like she and Shelby and I rehearsed earlier today in my office. "I'll call every single reporter in my phone.

Every single one of them. Some of them won't care, but the ones who do care? They'll dig up everything. Every. Single. Solitary. Thing."

"Okay," April says. She sighs. "I'll tell you what you want to know."

April leans toward Jules, so close that I bet Jules can smell her perfume.

She whispers something to Jules. Her long, shiny hair flops onto Jules's shoulder. Her lips come so close to touching Jules' ear that I wonder if her thick gloss left a mark.

She hastily pulls away from Jules and glances around the room. Her eyes land on Shelby. Then on me.

Oh, lord. Is our cover blown?

I feel like April's eyes are burning a hole in my body. I want to slide down the bar stool and take cover under the bar. But I also want to stand up and shout, 'Yes, bitch, look at me! Look at the real person whose life you're screwing with!'

April lifts her drink to her glossy mouth. "Cheers," she says to Jules.

Something about the glint in her eye is sinister. Something about the arch of her brows reads flirtatious.

"I'm going to cut to the chase," April says, "but first I'm going to need something from you."

"What makes you think you can get something from me," Jules asks.

"I'll tell you everything I know. On one condition."

"Who said this was a negotiation?"

"Trust me," April says, "trust me when I tell you that you're going to want to play ball. There's the scoop of a lifetime in it for you."

"I'm writing a story," Jules says. "I don't negotiate. Either you tell me what you know, or you don't."

"Okay, then," April says, "I guess you don't want me to confess? I guess you're not interested in what I have on Jimmy Montgomery?"

I could see in Jules' face that she was trying not to look desperate. She couldn't make any sudden moves. She looked at the tastefully polished concrete floor. After a pause, she said, in a tone she was clearly working hard to make condescending, "what is it that you want? I can't promise anything … above the fold."

"I want you to help me end Jimmy Montgomery," April says coolly, leaning in so close to Jules that she could certainly smell the liquor on her breath.

Jules can't hide the shock on her face.

"Relax," April says. "I don't want to murder him or anything. All I want is the death of his marriage and his public life."

"But why," Jules asks.

"I can't tell you that until you agree."

"I can't agree until you tell me."

"Then we've reached an impasse," April says, taking red lipstick out of her purse, applying it and smacking her lips together. It's like something out of a godawful Charlie's Angels movie.

"I guess we have," Jules says. She reaches for her Birkin and scoots out her chair to stand.

"Wait!" April says. "Just wait, okay?" Jules looks at April expectantly.

"I know you're not really a journalist," April says. "I know who you work for."

"I …" Jules clearly hadn't been prepared for this. I wished Shelby could feed her some lines. I wished we'd prepared for what to do if her cover was blown. "You're ridiculous," she says.

"That's absurd. Of course I'm a...."

"I guess you don't want to know why I tried to bring the Camdens down?" April asks. "I guess you're not interested in why I lied about your boss's husband?"

"I don't know what you're talking about," Jules says, still vaguely trying to play dumb. "Who the hell are the Camdens?"

"Drop it," April says. "Just drop it. You're a terrible actress." "I'm not act ...."

"I had to do it," April says, "I had to. Ted was supposed to take Jimmy Montgomery down. Ted was supposed to force Jimmy to resign, but then it seemed to me, rightly or wrongly, that Ted was going all soft on Jimmy and it might not happen and ..."

"Why?" Jules asks. "Why did you have to do it?"

"Because," April says, "because Lorelei wouldn't have left Jimmy on her own.

So I made a deal with the devil. He would leave Lorelei if I was able to get Ted Camden and the sexual harassment suit off his back. I thought if Jimmy left her, maybe she'd finally ..."

I was staring openly now at April's beautiful face, at her tarantula-like eyelashes, her contoured cheeks. It was a face contorted in pain. In the agony of unrequited love.

Shelby and I leave the Monocle and part ways at the Metro station. I watch Shelby walk away. She's probably going to spy on someone's good-for-nothing husband. Maybe I should have hired her to spy on mine and found out the story sooner.

I find Ted sacked out on the bed in nothing but his shorts snoring. ESPN is blaring full blast. It must be nice to be able to relax and then pass out! I fully intend to wake Ted up, but I find myself suddenly exhausted and stripping off my stupid disguise. I throw the wig on the floor and see Ted's t-shirt lying there in a pile. Usually, I'd have nagged him about that. I'm beat. I slip it on over my head. It smells like Old Spice and Ivory soap.

I lie gently on the bed and nuzzle into Ted's large, warm body. He wraps his arms around me in his sleep. When we were first married, we often slept this way. But then we had all those years of Kendall in our bed at night. It was a wonder we got any sleep with her body sprawled out between us. Then I started having hormone issues, which meant night sweats.

But here we are again. An image of Jules signaling for another drink comes to me. Another of April's silky hair. Go away. Surprisingly, the images obey. Ted's chest rises and falls with his snores. I close my eyes and try to time my breathing with his. For the first time in weeks, I feel myself drifting off to sleep, peacefully. I'm so tired. I imagine I can see Ted and me from above. All wrapped up in each other.

Chapter Eighteen

When I wake up in the morning, I know something is wrong. And not just because I've overslept. I look out the window of our house and see Shelby's car parked in my circular driveway next to a black BMW. The smell of coffee is rising from the kitchen. I pull on my sweats and sneakers and go downstairs.

Ted is standing at the bottom of the steps.

"Don't freak out," he says. "I know this is weird, but don't freak out. Calm down." Will he never learn that the two worst things someone can tell me are don't freak out and calm down?

"What the hell, Ted? You are freaking me out!"

He takes me by the hand and leads me into the living room.

That's when I see them. All four, arranged on our tasteful couches.

Jules.

Shelby.

Vivian.

And April.

Seeing the four of them together is surreal. Jules in her workout gear, clearly having interrupted her morning run for this meeting. Vivian in a pink Chanel suit, coiffed and made up at 10:30 a.m. on a Saturday. Shelby, demure as ever, and except for the shoes, a dead ringer for Candace Bergen in a Nancy Meyers movie. April, looking like a magazine cover model for shampoo, the recessed lighting glinting off her shiny mane. I want to reach out and touch it. She is beautiful. I could see why Ted wanted her. Her youth and her glow. Her nerve.

My husband, rocking a five o'clock shadow.

But this whole thing is feeling more Coen Brothers meets Lifetime thriller than airy beach town rom-com.

"Who wants to tell me what the hell is happening here," I ask. I can't shake the suspicion that I'm on a set — that none of this is real — as everyone starts chattering over each other at once. April talks with her hands, gesticulating wildly. Ted's voice is low and hesitant. Jules is using the tone she uses to set credit card companies straight. Shelby is muttering. Vivian is watching the scene with bright eyes.

I'm looking at all of them as if they're speaking in

five different foreign languages.

What the hell is happening? Why did I get out of bed?

A jolt of fear flows through my body as Shelby puts her finger in her mouth and lets out a shrill whistle.

"Oh my god," I mumble. This movie is getting weirder.

"Quiet," she says, and a hush falls over the living room. My living room. A woman my husband wanted to sleep with is in my living room. A woman who accused my husband of raping her is in my living room. One in the same.

I feel like I'm suffocating. It's so hot in here. April and Jules are on the loveseat together. Ted is halfway across the room, leaning against the built-ins that hold our books. A whole marriage worth of books. He's as far as he can get from April while still being in the same room, yet I'm overcome with the urge to put even more distance between them. To put myself in between them. I know it's dumb, but I want to knock her down and kick her away from my husband like she's some kind of wild animal trying to maul him.

"April," Shelby says, "you go first."

April clears her throat. I watch the bones in her long, thin neck twitch with the motion. She licks her full lips. "Well," she says, "hello, Elaine."

Hearing her voice saying my name in my living room is too much. I feel like the walls are closing in on me and I know that if I don't get out of there, I'm going to flip out.

April looks me in the eye. The nerve of her! The chutzpah!

I start to back away. I have no idea why Shelby or Ted or Jules or anyone thought it was a good idea to bring this group together in my home without my knowledge. Is this their idea of some sort of intervention of the cast of characters presently in my life?

I don't think so.

I turn around and make a break for the door. I'm grateful for the sneakers I'm wearing. Then, I bolt.

I start running. I don't know where I'm going but I have to get away from this room. From these people. From this house.

I run to the end of the driveway and onto Park Street. I can hear Ted yelling for me from the door. He'd probably pass out if he tried to chase me.

"Leave me alone," I yell.

I run to the light at Belle View and then onto King Street. My lungs are burning, and my thighs are burning. I haven't run in years, but, still, I run. Wearing this sweat suit, which I now realize I've never actually sweated in, I could be any of the suburban white ladies jogging through the quaint streets of Old Town on a quiet weekend morning. I look behind me, half expecting to see Ted in the car, but I don't. I run past the wine shop and the spice shop and the newsstand and the coffee bar. I watch my feet in my mint green sneakers with the pink swoosh clapping against the gray sidewalk.

I feel a little like I'm flying. No one comes after me.

I only make it as far as the park, a few blocks from home, where I used to push Kendall's stroller in an endless loop during her colic phase. I huff and puff over to a bench. I'm burning up, despite the prickle of cold in the air. I put my head between my knees. The wave of nausea passes. My calf muscles pulse. I need to rest.

I scan my surroundings and notice a children's soccer game in progress on the field a few paces away. Kendall loved this park. Soccer was her passion. I'm overwhelmed by the desire to join the game, to kick a ball with all my might and watch it sail past the chunky boy playing goalie, smacking the net with a delicious whoosh.

I get up and walk toward the game, feeling a rivulet of sweat trickle down my back. I smile at the parents yelling, remembering the years I spent juggling my work calendar in order to be present for Kendall's games. My gaze falls on a towheaded blonde child in a purple jersey moving deftly down the field, zigging and zagging to avoid the yellow jerseys closing in on him. He pulls his right foot back and kicks. The ball sails through the air and past the goalie.

"Go, Jamesie," the children begin to shout.

"Nice job! Way to go, big guy," yells a woman, presumably his mother.

Three pale blonde children, one of them no more than a year old, toddle towards the little boy, and clobber him with hugs and high fives.

"Jamesie," they yell, "Yay, Jamesie!"

Jamesie, I think. Why do I know that name? Then, I remember.

My brain fills with the memory of Senator Montgomery, sliding his phone across the table slyly, proud of the four perfect tots decades younger than the children from his previous marriage.

I knew Senator Montgomery lived on Capitol Hill as so many Senators do. But Lorelei? Why would she be here now? This doesn't make sense.

Then, before I can stop myself, I'm running. Again. What is it about this situation that makes my body feel so out of my control? This time, I'm running toward the children and the woman.

Lorelei? It must be. The fear of being wrong once more gives me pause. I am terrified.

I don't care about the stink of my sweat, my face without makeup. I know I must look godawful. But I don't care.

The ref blows the whistle and the team is back on the field again, their tiny legs clad in impossibly cute knee socks carrying them up and down the sidelines. This time, Jamesie is sitting on the bench, giving some other child a chance to shine.

What the hell am I doing?

Good question.

I take a deep breath. I tap Lorelei Montgomery, or at least the woman I think is her, on the shoulder.

She turns around. Yes, it's her. "Hi," she says, a puzzled smile spreading across her face. I notice with shock that she is exceedingly too young for her husband. "Did you need something?"

"I need to talk to you," I say. "It's about your husband. It's about April."

I expect her to slap me, but she doesn't. She nods. She hands the smallest of her children off to the nanny. "I need a few minutes, Olga," she says.

She picks up two folding camp chairs and hands

me one of them. She walks away from the game and I follow. Together, we sit.

"I'm Ela…"

"I know who you are," she says. She does?

"What is it that you need to know," she asks.

"Everything," I tell her.

She stares at me for what seems like an eternity.

"Well," she says, "it's complicated."

'That's the understatement of the year', I think, and then Lorelei starts talking, her story unfolding like a caged animal finally being set free.

April had never had boyfriends, Lorelei tells me. She was tall and awkward, only blossoming into a shiny-haired bombshell in college. She was shy and unsure of her beauty and seemed to shrink in on herself whenever she got attention for it. She was whip smart and bookish. Hermione Granger, basically. She had big ambitions. April McFarland was going to be the first woman senator from Virginia.

Lorelei, on the other hand, used her beauty. She was a pageant queen, and she'd had boyfriends since her parents began allowing her to group date at fifteen. At seventeen at church camp, she'd had her first kiss. She'd been careful not to let it go further than lips on lips, no tongue. But her heart was never in it, with boys.

Lorelei's parents were hard-core evangelicals, so she'd taken one of those purity pledges. As a Southern Baptist, she didn't drink. She didn't smoke. She lived by the adage 'modest is hottest'. Her youth group spent weekends picking up garbage, volunteering at soup kitchens, and protesting outside Planned Parenthood.

A few months before school started, April and Lorelei discovered that they'd be roommates at UVA. They'd both been nervous, but they'd talked on the phone for half an hour and had become fast friends despite their differences. For weeks prior to their move to Charlottesville, they chatted on the phone late into the night, often falling asleep with their cordless phones in their hands.

Together, they pledged a sorority. They spent every waking moment together. One night, April convinced Lorelei to go out drinking at a bar that wouldn't card them.

That's when it started.

"We got knee-walking drunk," Lorelei says. "I'd never even tasted alcohol."

On the way back up to their room, they'd stopped in the stairwell for a rest.

April leaned her head on Lorelei's shoulder.

"I remember smelling her hair," Lorelei says. "And,

well, I can't believe I'm telling this to a stranger, but it was like electricity went through my whole body, and I knew that I loved her like a girl is supposed to love a boy."

They'd kissed. They'd done much more. "Much more than I'm going to go into," Lorelei says. "Suffice it to say: we've loved each other since then. Since the beginning, actually. But I couldn't tell my parents."

Lorelei glanced over at the children.

"We've had to keep it secret," she says. "There was no way we could be together, you see."

"I don't really see," I say, "why couldn't you just ..."

"My father is a preacher," she says. "My father would sooner see me dead than ..." She looks at the ground.

They'd continued to see each other all through college. When April moved to Cambridge for law school, Lorelei followed. There, in a new city in a faraway state, they could be together in the open. They could hold hands at dinner. "Then my mother got sick," Lorelei says. "I came back to Virginia to take care of her. She had breast cancer. After her chemo was over, we had a big party. Jimmy came. I had too much to drink, and he kept trying to get me alone and, well, I felt bad for him because his wife had just passed and I ... well, you know the rest," she says.

I glance at the soccer field, at little Jamesie running up and down the field. "Your parents made you marry him?"

"Well," she says, "part of me wanted to, part of me thought that it would just go away — all these things I felt for April. I went back to Boston, and I packed. I left her."

Lorelai's eyes, framed by the same spiderlike lashes as April's, fill with tears.

"How did she take it?" I ask. I touch her arm, gently. This is so unreal.

"She shut me out. I'd call to check on her and she'd let it go to voicemail.

Then my mom and I were doing invitations for my baby shower."

I remember the picture. April's hands cradling Lorelei's baby bump.

Lorelei's mother had sent April an invitation. She didn't RSVP. But she showed up with a six-tiered diaper cake. When Lorelei opened the door, she threw her arms around April. She had talked herself into believing that her marriage had undone all of the feelings she'd had for April. She'd told herself that the marriage and the baby that was coming had undone 'all that business in Boston'. She'd leaned into her Southern Baptist roots, her deep knowledge of 'the Lord's word'. Her baby and her husband were a gift from the Lord, a sign that she wasn't 'one of those lesbians'.

But.

Then she saw April.

"I couldn't bear to be apart from her," Lorelei said. "When I went on tour for the book, she came with me."

I want to laugh out loud at the idea of an evangelical anti-choice 'preborn advocate' on book tour with her lesbian lover, but I don't. I actually feel sorry for Lorelei. I actually feel sympathy for April, too. Suddenly, she seems almost human.

Then one night, April had come over for a movie night after the kids went to bed.

"One thing led to another. We fell asleep on the bed in a compromising position. We were all curled up together and then I woke up to Jimmy screaming. He was furious. He called us … " her voice drops to a low whisper, "the d-word."

I feel a hand on my shoulder. I turn to find it's Shelby's.

"Elaine," she says. "Come on, everyone's waiting."

Shelby pauses, considers Lorelei, who she knew had been in the park anticipating April's return from this morning's meeting.

"You'd better come along now too, I suppose."

Chapter Nineteen

If I thought it was strange to see Jules, April, Ted, Vivian and Shelby in my living room, it was even stranger to add Lorelei to the mix.

Ever the beauty queen, Lorelai crossed her legs at the ankle when she took a seat next to April on the settee. I focused on their hands now intertwined. They were wearing the same color nail polish.

"So spell it out for me," Ted says. "Explain to me exactly why it is you decided to go ahead and ruin my life."

April talks. Shelby pours everyone coffee. She pulls a flask out of her purse and passes it around. Vivian, I am delighted to see, pours a healthy shot into her cup.

It started with the night that Senator Montgomery found Lorelei and April in bed. He went on a rampage, yanking drawers open and throwing Lorelei's clothes into a large trunk they used for overseas travel.

He hissed homophobic slurs at them.

"You good-for-nothing lesbian whores," he yelled.

We can all imagine him screaming this in his drawl. His tan jowls shaking in anger. His fire-and-brimstone preacher roots yanked to the surface by anger.

April treats us to an impersonation of Senator Jimmy Montgomery so faithful that it would be hilarious if it weren't so tragic. "They'll fucking crucify me for this, goddammit," she yelled, playing him. "My career will never recover. A fucking lesbo for a wife. Them neo-Nazi boys will be on their damn message boards calling me a 'cuck.' I won't have it, Lorelei. I won't goddamn have it. I've worked too hard. And that damn sexual harassment case."

"He says it like 'hair-ess-mint,'" April tells us. "That's where I got the idea, I think. When he said that, a little light bulb just lit up in my brain."

The night that Senator Montgomery found his wife in bed with her college roommate was the same night Ted and I were making pasta carbonara in our kitchen. As the bacon fried in our old cast iron skillet, I'd been seething. As April McFarland's plot to take down her lover's husband had only just begun to form, I grew increasingly irritated with my husband. How dare Ted consider taking on the case against Senator Montgomery? How dare he!

Now, hearing April unspool the threads of this

insane plot, I wonder if my anger that night wasn't some kind of premonition. Maybe on some cosmic level I understood that things were going to go badly.

"He told me he was going to take my children," Lorelei says. "He told me I'd never be able to see them again. He'd tell them that Mommy was sick and diseased."

"He's the one who's sick and diseased," April says. She says it pointedly to Lorelai, as if she's trying to convince her that what they're doing isn't wrong. That it's okay for them to love each other.

Once again, my feelings toward April change. I feel myself softening to her. In her, I see Kendall. I see myself. I see Little Lainey Bower. I remember falling for Ted, loving him so deeply and ferociously. What if someone had made me feel ashamed of that? What if someone had told me that my feelings weren't natural? What if I'd had to watch Ted marry someone else? Have child after child with her? It would have killed me. Suddenly, I want to cradle April McFarland in my arms.

"So, we had to bargain," Lorelei says.

"That's where you came in, Ted," April says. She stands and moves toward where Ted is sitting on the sectional. She reaches for his shoulder. Even though I know that April has no feeling for my husband, the thought of her touching him stings.

"Don't," Ted says, shrugging his body away from her. "Do not touch me."

I move closer to him. I put my arms around him protectively, feeling his body relax into mine.

"Back up the story, babe," Lorelei says. "Remember? He came home and went crazy and threw all my things at the trunk. He was going to kick me out right then and there, the way I'd always been afraid my parents would be if they found out that I'm ...."

"Gay," I say. Lorelei winces.

"He was going to divorce me and take my kids. But then he said that thing about the harassment case."

"It was like you could see him realizing how bad it would look to get a divorce in the middle of it. His face went white, and he started taking everything out of the trunk," April says. "I was getting dressed and trying to make my exit."

"But then he just zeroed in on her," Lorelei says. Her eyes well with tears. "For a minute, I thought he might hurt her. Or worse. I started thinking, shit, where are the guns? You know he's one of them NRA good ol' boys."

"They've given him enough money," I mumble.

"Exactly," says April.

He looks at her and he just says 'You'.

"It was quite menacing," April says.

He said that April was forbidden from ever entering the Montgomery home again. If she so much as text messaged Lorelei, he'd divorce Lorelei and make her life a living hell.

He said, "If I get even a whiff of contact between you, I'll take those kids, Lor, and I swear it. You'll never see them again. I'll tell your mama and daddy what deviance I saw right here in my own bed. They'll ship you off to one of those conversion camps. Hell, they're liable to have you committed, knowing them."

"He grabbed my arm so hard it left bruises," April says. "He told us we had five minutes to say our final good-byes."

I could imagine them there in that room. Two beautiful young women. One man with an old, worn-out kind of handsomeness.

"I thought I was going to die," Lorelei says. She begins to sob. "Choosing between my babies and my parents and the love of my life." April smooths Lorelei's hair.

"It's okay," April says, "it's okay. I'm here now. I'm not going anywhere."

"Can we get to the point where you decided to ruin my marriage and my career," Ted asks. I've softened, and he's hardened. I can feel the heat of his rage. I don't blame him for being mad.

April swallows hard and nods.

She tells us that she began to beg Senator Montgomery not to do this. She pleaded with him to let them continue as things were. She begged him to divorce Lorelei. She floated the suggestion, desperately, that she could become the live-in nanny. She even promised that both she and Lorelei would sleep with him.

"I told him I'd do anything. I sobbed. I groveled. I told him I'd do anything. Please, Senator," I said, "I'll do anything. You name it and I'll do it. Please just don't take her away."

"And me, I was just curled up in the fetal position on the bed," Lorelei says. "soaking those high thread count sheets with my miserable tears."

"Then the senator sits down on the edge of the bed," April says. "He closes his eyes and massages his temples. Without warning, rage just seems to wash over him again. He hurls a remote control at the wall."

Then he yells, "Goddamnit, I'd love to be rid of you. I'd just love to be rid of this," he shouts. But he knows he can't get a divorce with this harassment case going on. How would that look?

April tells us that's when she stepped in. She took a deep breath. She asked him what she had to do to make that case go away. What if she could, she said? What if?

"If you can make this harassment bullshit go away," Senator Montgomery says to April, "hell, then you can have her. Free and clear."

That's when April went to work on Ted. All those years of being undercover for her gossip blog meant she knew her way in and out of DC circles. She called in a favor to her dad's friend Pete, who introduced her to Ted. She wore a sexy-but-not-too-sexy outfit to the interview. She impressed Ted with her insider knowledge of Senator Montgomery.

"Remind me to kill Pete next time I see him," Ted says, exasperated.

The case against him, as she soon realized, was airtight. He was unequivocally guilty of discrimination, and he was going to pay through the nose. April was smart. She was in love. She was resourceful.

The way she saw it, she had two options. She could take down Senator Montgomery, or she could do as she promised and take down the case against him. She'd much rather do the former than the latter. She would have found it much more satisfying to see the man ruined.

So she went first to the depositions, looking for any hint that Senator Montgomery might have done something worse than being a sexist old jackass. Specifically, she went looking for a woman who might accuse him of rape.

"It turned out, though, that the worst he'd done was harass these women. Fire them. Say sexist things. Hold them back professionally. Discrimination isn't sexy enough to cause a real maelstrom in Washington, as you know," April says. "I mean, it didn't look good, that's for sure. I knew he was going to pay through the nose. I knew his donors weren't going to like it. I knew he was mad as hell that these 'little women' had the nerve to fight for their rights. But it wasn't the kind of career-ending resignation letter that would be the ruin that I was looking for."

Unable to find sufficient dirt on Senator Montgomery, she went after Ted's case against him. Unfortunately for April, the case was airtight, clear-cut, open-and-shut. He would surely lose, and it was going to cost him a fortune and probably his career. April explains that she was down to her last resort: if she couldn't poke holes in Ted's case, she'd have to poke holes in Ted. If she couldn't find a woman to accuse Senator Montgomery of rape, she'd have to find a woman who would instead accuse the big-shot litigator defending the case. Hell, she'd have to be that woman.

"Are you fucking kidding me right now, April?" Ted screams. "I fucking trusted you."

I'm torn between wanting to sympathize with my husband for feeling betrayed and feeling betrayed myself.

April had been the one who started coming on to Ted.

"Spare me the details," I say. "Please fucking spare me. I don't want to know any more about what you did. I want to figure out how we're going to undo this."

"We have a proposal," says Jules.

"We?" I ask.

"Vivian and I," she says.

Vivian waves her fingers at us, grinning.

"We put our heads together," she says.

"It was supposed to be our Plan B," Jules tells us.

"Not anymore, sweetie," Vivian says. "Now it's our Plan A."

An hour later, my living room is full of staff from MSNBC. Vivian knew exactly what to do and who to call. She still carried weight with the media. Viv wanted action and this was a scoop no station could pass up.

The technicians wired all of us. This is it. We're doing it.

The producer sticks his hand between us and the camera, counting down. "And we're live in 5-4-3-2-1."

Our tell-all begins with Lorelai.

"I've been living a lie." she says. "But I'm tired of hiding. It's time for me to tell the truth. It's time for me to be transparent."

"Me, too," says April McFarland.

"Me, too," I say.

Together, we tell the world what we know. That Senator Montgomery is abundantly a liar, a cheat, a homophobe, a serial discriminator, a crabby old man, and a master manipulator.

"Time's up, Senator Montgomery," April says to the camera. "It's time for the people of this great nation to understand the kind of man who's representing them and take steps to correct that problem."

"My husband has repeatedly shamed me just for being who I am," adds Lorelai. "He's threatened to take away the people I love most in this world — my children — because he preaches a kind of bigoted Christianity that doesn't take into account that God loves us all, just as we are."

I look squarely into the camera.

"I met Senator Montgomery earlier this year for a drink, and he told me that he'd only approve my confirmation for federal judgeship if I rescinded my belief that every woman should be able to choose if, when, how, and how many times she becomes a mother. I want to tell all Americans today that there is no job that is more important than your values. I want to say that, whether I continue to approach the bench or whether I serve from the bench, I will continue to be a champion for women." I gesture to April and Lorelai. "I will fight for all women to be free to make their own decisions about their bodies."

We continue talking, explaining our shared experiences as women, and I'm finally asked a question about my candidacy as a federal judge. I open my mouth to respond, and there's a racket behind me as someone slams a door and apparently knocks over a microphone stand. All heads swivel away from me and focus on the hubbub.

It's Vivian. "Elaine!" she says, waving a cell phone at me. "You have a call." "Viv," I say. What the hell? What would ever in a million years possess my public relations wizard, my political advisor, my feminist hero of a mother-in-law, to interrupt me while I'm giving an interview on national television?

"Apparently you've been ignoring your phone," she says, walking right past the cameras, onto the television set they've made of my living room. She hands me my phone. "Your poor daughter has been worried sick."

"Vivian," I whisper, knowing my mic is still live anyway so what's the point, "can't this wait?" If only she knew how good I really am at avoiding my daughter's calls. For two days I've been meaning to call her; I still hadn't gotten around to filling her in on everything that's happened, including my reunion with her father. I felt guilty. I suppose Vivian would never in her life fail to return a call from her child. But still: in the middle of an interview? Really?

"Would you please let her know I'll call her right back," I ask Vivian.

"No," she replies. She thrusts the phone into my hands. I shrug an apology to the reporter and the others, who are looking at me with concern. "Kendall?" I say into the phone.

"Mom!" she cries. "Where have you been? Why haven't you answered your phone, for chrissake?"

"Sweetie, I've been a little bit busy. I'll explain everything–"

"Where are you," she demands.

"I'm at home, Kendall! There are reporters—"

"Mom," she interrupts. "Mom!"

"What?"

"Inhale."

"Inhale? Okay." I inhale. Everyone watches.

"Okay?" Kendall says.

"Kendall! What is it?"

"I'm in labor, Mama," she says. "Contractions coming–"

Through the telephone I hear my sweet girl, her voice amplified with intense beautiful rhythmic grunting sounds.

I leap off the couch and I'm through the door with Ted at my heels, and we screech away from the house and are halfway to the hospital before I realize I'm still wearing my microphone.

Epilogue

On a blustery cold but sunny day, I don my favorite eggplant shift dress. I walk up the steps of the capitol, surrounded by friends and family.

I place my hand on the Bible as the Vice President swears me in as a federal judge. I promise to uphold the Constitution, and I mean it.

"Reservation for Judge Elaine Bower-Camden," I tell the host at the Monocle.

"Congratulations, ma'am," he replies professionally, and leads me to their back dining room, where generations of congressmembers and senators and judges and mayors have come together after hard-fought campaigns to celebrate their victories and commiserate their defeats. I look around. The room is full of people who care about me. Ted, of course, and Vivian, holding onto him and looking frail. She had a hard fall on her front porch steps last month and spent a few days in the hospital, making us appreciate her presence among us all the more. Kendall sits front and center, left breast out, nursing my perfect baby granddaughter, named Vivvy for her great-grandma. Shelby occupies a corner, whistling and stamping her feet like a Teamster. Jules is in the back, video recording the proceedings on her cell phone. She'll come with me to my new job, of course, as my chief federal court judicial assistant. And my friend.

"Speech," someone shouts – Jules, I'm pretty certain, disguising her voice – and the crowd joins in, jostling me toward the center of the room.

"Thank you." I go into talking-head mode, saying kind things about people, sharing my values, making self-deprecating jokes. The crowd is warm, and receptive, and because I'm in a room full of people who love me, they'd be that way no matter what I say. Lorelei and April are clapping louder than anyone, hooting and woo-hooing at every sentence. Lorelei's kids are jumping around the room, a quartet of blonde hellions.

I'm wrapping up my comments, having nothing much more to add to the general happy mood, my heart as full as it's been for as long as I can remember. But I am overcome with a wave of emotion at the sight of Elena Morales walking through the door, and behind her is Sammy. Sadly, it will be longer for Sally. She will be released in eighteen months.

"Oh!" I cry aloud, delighted and gobsmacked and

taken completely off guard, "look who it is!"

All heads in the room swivel toward the door, just as I realize maybe these two ex-convicts would prefer not to be stared at by all these people. But I can't help it; I'm so happy to see them. "Sorry!" I say to Elena and Sammy, and in an attempt to rescue them from the unwanted attention, I blurt out that they're old friends, and I'm just so glad they came, and I start to tell people to enjoy the food and drink, and don't forget to tip the bartender–

"Wait," says Elena Morales, in a voice that is strong and confident. "Can I say a few words?"

She makes her way to the front of the room and pulls out a piece of paper. "This lady," she says to the room, gesturing nervously in my direction, "saved my life."

"No," I protest, "really–"

"Mine, too!" yells Sammy.

"Seriously, I was just doing my job–" I tell everyone.

Elena, however, is not done talking. She shows me her palm and shakes the notes in her hand dramatically.

"Shut up, your honor," she says, and the crowd roars with laughter.

ACKNOWLEDGEMENTS

My gratitude and thanks are extended to those individuals who helped me with their advice, wisdom, and encouragement. If anyone has been excluded from these lists, it is clearly unintentional.

These people assisted me in every way possible, above and beyond the bonds of friendship and love. I remain indebted for the continual kindness they showed me in making this book a reality: Shannon Cain, Mary Lawrence, Suzanne Rabe, Elizabeth Smith, Jessica Teel and Penny Waterstone.

Additionally, these individuals helped by either reading, editing or just listening to me convey my thoughts and ideas: Karen Christiansen, Eve M. Hady, Margy McGonagill, Stephanie Parker, Vera Pfeuffer, Mary Ann Pressman, Peg Schmidt, Neil Sechan, Gretchen Shine and Deborah Steinberg.

Book Cover Design: Anthony Ruggiero
Graphic Designer